North Town

LORENZ GRAHAM

North Town

Foreword by Rudine Sims Bishop
Afterword by Ruth Graham Siegrist

Boyds Mills Press

Published by Boyds Mills Press, Inc.
A Highlights Company
815 Church Street
Honesdale, Pennsylvania 18431
Printed in China

Publisher Cataloging-in-Publication Data (U.S.)

Publisher Cataloging-in-Publication Data (U.S.)

Graham, Lorenz B.
    North Town / Lorenz Graham ; foreword by Rudine Sims Bishop. —1st ed.
[192] p. : cm.
Originally published: NY: Thomas Y. Crowell Company, 1976.
Summary: David Williams, newly arrived from a small town in the south, encounters racial prejudice in a northern city.
ISBN 1-59078-162-7
1. African Americans—Fiction. 2. Race relations—Fiction. I. Bishop, Rudine Sims .
II. Title.
    [F] 21   2003
2002117200

First Boyds Mills Press edition, 2003
The text of this book is set in 12-point Palatino.

Visit our Web site at www.boydsmillspress.com

10 9 8 7 6 5 4 3 2 1 hc

To my daughter, Jean Graham Jones,
and to her daughter, Stephanie

Foreword

Lorenz Graham believed with all his heart that "people are people." That statement seems obvious on the face of it, but behind it is a lifetime conviction fed by both happy and unhappy experiences with people in many places in the world, and by a strong religious faith. When Graham was twenty-two years old, he dropped out of college in California to become a missionary in Monrovia, Liberia, in Africa. Before he left the United States, he had read and been told many things about what Africans would be like. People used words like "savages" and "heathens" and "uncivilized," and warned him of danger. At first he carried a weapon when he went out at night, but he soon discovered that he was "safer on a dark trail in Africa at midnight than [he] would have been on a well-lighted street in an American city." He learned that Africans were very much like the people he had known in the United States—ordinary people living ordinary lives. It was that experience in Africa and in France, where he spent some time recuperating from malaria, that made him decide to become a writer,

> with the one message that "People are People—white, black and all shades and colors between, African, American, French, German. The cultures of the world, and the conflicts when we who call ourselves people refuse to recognize that those whom we call enemies are also people, very much like ourselves, with desires, needs and hopes which are quite identical to our own desires and needs and hopes.

When he later wrote a book about an African boy and his adventures in daily living, he was very pleased when a newspaper reviewer wrote that an American reader would recognize the African boy as "just another fellow." That was exactly what Graham had hoped for. In the context of the United States of his day, Graham's idea that "people are people" had an added meaning. Not only did he want his readers to understand that people the world over are basically alike, he wanted them to understand that all people are deserving of basic human rights and social justice. He wanted to say through his novels that all people have a right to equal treatment under the law and the right to "life, liberty, and the pursuit of happiness" as stated in the United States Declaration of Independence.

Lorenz Graham's four "Town" novels—*South Town*, *North Town*, *Whose Town?*, and *Return to South Town*—not only relate the story of David Williams and his odyssey from a small rural southern town to the North and back again, but also chronicle the turbulence and social change that took place from the mid-1950s through the end of the 1960s. These novels are set at a time when social conditions were grim for many African Americans, especially in the South. In spite of those conditions, however, people like the Williams family and their neighbors tried to live ordinary lives in places like South Town. They went to church and worked hard and tried to see that their children would grow up to enjoy better lives. Although they sometimes were forced to give in to some of the discriminatory customs of the day in order to survive, they always held onto their sense of dignity and refused to lose hope. Sometimes, conditions became unbearable, and some families packed up and moved to the North, where life was in some ways better, but where different problems awaited them. This was the era of the mid-century Civil Rights Movement; and reading these novels about an ordinary, but in some ways extraordinary, African American family reminds us not only why that movement was necessary but also how difficult the struggle has been.

It is hard to imagine what life must have been like in the rural South in the mid-1950s, but perhaps a look even farther back in time will help. History tells us that for more than two hundred years, between 1619 and 1865, most Black people in the South had been enslaved. One excuse some people had made up to justify slavery was that Africans or Black people were inferior to white people—not as smart, not as capable, in fact not quite as high up on the ladder of humanity. Therefore, these white supremacists believed, Black people did not deserve the same rights as whites. Even after the Civil War and the emancipation of Black people, even though the Constitution was amended to make Black Americans citizens with the right to vote, even a hundred years later and beyond, many white supremacists held on to those antiquated and false ideas.

So, especially in small rural towns in the South, "Jim Crow" laws, or segregation laws, were still affecting daily life in the 1950s. Back in 1896, the Supreme Court had ruled that it was legal to separate people by race, provided the separate facilities were "equal." Even though "black" and "white" facilities were never really equal, Black and white people were forced to live separate daily lives: separate water fountains, separate waiting rooms at bus or train stations, separate schools. And invariably the "black" or "colored"—as they were called then—facilities were inferior. *South Town* is set just after the Supreme Court of the United States had declared that "separate but equal" schools were inherently unequal, and had ordered the states to desegregate their schools "with all deliberate speed." But it would take years for that ruling to take hold and make a practical difference.

Furthermore, even when segregationist practices were not written into law, they were "understood." In *South Town*, for instance, it was understood that white boys and Black boys would not swim in the same place in the stream at the same time; when one group arrived, the other would leave. Black people were not permitted to eat at "white" restaurants or lunch counters, or try on clothes in department stores, or ride in the front seats of buses or trains. White store clerks would not touch Black people's hands as they exchanged money in stores. There are numerous examples of the kind of humiliation Black people faced every day.

Possibly worst of all, white supremacists expected Black people to kowtow to them. It was considered an act of defiance for Black people to look white people straight in the eyes. If a white person and a Black person passed each other on the sidewalk, the Black person was expected to step off into the street. And Black people were not expected to "talk back" to white people. These practices were often backed up by the full force of local law-enforcement personnel. A prominent white person could have any Black person arrested for disobeying one of these unwritten "laws." White supremacists also used violence, as well as fear and intimidation tactics, such as burning down houses, to keep Black people "in their place." In many cases, this system worked because Black sharecroppers lived on land owned by whites and were dependent on the landowners, who were also the store owners and farm equipment suppliers, to keep a roof over their heads and food on their tables.

It is clear throughout these novels that part of Lorenz Graham's belief that "people are people" was the conviction that, in any group and under any social system, there are people with good hearts and the courage to treat others with kindness and dignity, even if doing so puts themselves at risk. And so, even though many of the white characters in these novels are bad actors, there are also white characters who do the right thing and who befriend or defend the Williams family in times of crisis. And, Graham makes clear, there are Black people who are bad actors as well.

The second and third novels in the series are set in the North. In *North Town*, David and his family have moved, in part because they had been so victimized in South Town that David's father could no longer make a living, and in part so that David could have access to an education that would better prepare him for medical school. His ambition is to become a physician and return to South Town to serve the people there. *Whose Town?* chronicles the Williams's second year in the North, when David is a senior in high school. (Although *South Town* appears to be set in the mid-1950s, and *Whose Town?* is supposedly two years beyond their move to the North, there appears to be some discrepancy in actual time setting. In *Whose Town?*, for example, Graham mentions the assassination of Dr. Martin Luther King, which took place in 1968, the year before *Whose Town?* was published. By moving the time forward, Graham is able to weave a more dramatic, and at the time more contemporary, backdrop into the stories.)

The two North Town books provide a picture of some of the

complexities of living in the North, and in large cities generally, in the late 1950s and 1960s. Although the social conditions in the North were not as bad for African Americans as they were in the South, and although the schools were not legally segregated by race, there were still bigotry and racism to contend with. All over America, African Americans were standing up in an organized way to demand social justice. In the South, the Civil Rights Movement was in full swing. In December 1955, Mrs. Rosa Parks's refusal to give up her seat on a bus had sparked the Montgomery, Alabama, bus boycott, and the rise to prominence of Dr. Martin Luther King, Jr. Dr. King and his followers preached nonviolence as a way to confront unjust conditions and to bring about change. Marches, sit-ins, and freedom rides challenged Jim Crow laws all over the South. In 1963, there was a massive March on Washington for Jobs and Freedom. "We Shall Overcome" became the anthem of the Civil Rights Movement.

Not everyone agreed that nonviolence was the best strategy for addressing African Americans' grievances. Many African Americans thought that people should protect their rights "by any means necessary." Sometimes actions were not organized, but exploded out of frustration with particular incidents or in response to conditions that simply became unbearable. In such cities as Los Angeles in 1965 and Detroit in 1967, some African Americans set fires and looted stores in their own neighborhoods out of frustration and rage. Not surprisingly, within African American communities there was often debate over how best to right the wrongs that African Americans had suffered for so long. The two North Town novels explore the range of attitudes and behaviors that were prevalent among both Black and white citizens, and place David and his family in positions that force them to grapple with the issues and decide what is the right thing for them to do; the right way for them to behave.

In the final book of the series, *Return to South Town*, David is completing his medical training and is fulfilling his dream of returning to his home town to set up practice in the community. The South has changed dramatically, but some of the people he knew when he was a teenager in South Town are still there, and their attitudes have not changed. Nevertheless, in the New South David finds friends, both Black and white, who are willing and able to help him overcome obstacles, and who bring home to him once again the fact that "people are people."

In many ways, Lorenz Graham was a pioneer. When the first three of his Town novels were published, there were very few honest, realistic books for young people about African American families. In that regard, Graham helped to pave the way for the development of contemporary African American literature for children and young adults. It was not easy to be a pioneer. If he had had his way, *South Town* would have been published years earlier. Even though it was based on his experiences living and working in Virginia, it took years for him to convince a publisher that his African American characters were true to life. But he persevered and refused to compromise the truth as he knew it. The books were pioneering, too, in their confrontation of the racist practices he knew existed in communities all over the nation.

It seems especially fitting that I complete this foreword on the one hundred and first anniversary of Lorenz Graham's birth. (He was born on January 27, 1902.) I had the privilege of meeting him on a couple of occasions, and he impressed me as a kind and gentle man with immense inner strength. The sincerity and depth of his belief in the ultimate triumph of social justice shines through his novels even today, more than forty years after the first one was published. He has left a priceless legacy, and it is my hope that these novels will provoke a new generation of readers to consider the authenticity of Graham's belief that "people are people," and the ways our world might change if we all acted on that belief.

Rudine Sims Bishop
Professor Emerita
The Ohio State University

North Town

David Williams was going to school in North Town for the first time. He was alone and he was colored, a newcomer from the South. Sixteen years old and reaching for six feet, he was neatly dressed, his dark brown skin washed clean and his crinkly hair pressed down as tight as he could get it. He thought that people would know he was new and be watching him. He was not sure what he was supposed to do, for he had never gone to a school with white students. He had never ridden on a bus where colored passengers were not separated from white. That was why he was walking this morning.

Groups of boys and girls were walking in the same direction, and he looked at them curiously. He was also watching to see how they looked at him. He wished he'd see a colored fellow he could join. The white boys did not seem unfriendly. No one laughed at him or made unkind remarks; they seemed not to notice him at all.

He had walked all the way from the Williams family's new home on East Sixth Street. He was wearing his good wool suit, and he felt uncomfortably warm, even though it was the first day of October. Last evening his father had shown him where to get the bus and where to get off it a block from the North Town Central High School, but David had chosen to start early and to walk.

As he came in sight of the school, he suddenly realized that it would be the largest building he had ever entered. Probably all the people of his hometown would fit into it at one time, he thought. Built of handsome light-colored brick and stone with a central tower, it reminded him of a great church or castle. Students were moving toward its doors from all directions. Greetings were exchanged, and David caught scraps of conversation. Some students hurried, but many lingered as though unwilling to give up their freedom.

Nearby in front of a candy store a crowd of boys, some of them smoking, filled the sidewalk. Clowning, they jostled two girls, forcing them to step off the curb into the street. As David approached, trying not to look as though he expected trouble, he heard a loud outburst of laughter. He did not slow down but went on, his eyes straight ahead, though he was afraid someone might strike him from behind. There was a quick scuffle on his right. Two or three bodies smashed hard against him, spinning him across the walk and into a metal newspaper rack.

"Look out!" someone shouted.

David caught his balance just short of the curb. He straightened up and looked around angrily. He could not fight the whole crowd, but he was ready and willing to take them on one by one. But the boys who had shoved him were already running toward the school. The other students laughed as they watched a stout man in a white apron come out of the store to collect the newspapers that lay in disorder on the sidewalk.

"Juvenile delinquents, Daddy!" one of the boys taunted.

David did not join in the laughter. He was not amused and he wanted to avoid trouble. He had expected some of the white boys to be mean, and he determined grimly he would be watching for them and ready to fight any time he had to.

He walked on, but now the school seemed less beautiful. It looked more like a fort than a church.

A bell was ringing as he started up the wide steps. It was not late, but he started running, taking the steps two at a time. He slowed as he neared the door. Some other colored students were going in, but they did not notice him, and inside the building everyone seemed to be in a hurry. Not wanting to draw attention to himself, David tried to act as though he knew where to go and what to do. He turned to the right and walked down the hall.

There, along the wall, was a large glass case filled with athletic trophies—silver cups, bronze plaques, and statuettes of runners and players. He stopped and studied the inscriptions. North Town Central High seemed to hold championships in nearly every sport.

There were photographs of the winning teams, too. Studying the picture of a baseball team, he thought he saw some colored boys, though caps partly covered their faces and he could not be sure. But in the first row of a football photo there was definitely one dark fellow, his jersey pulled tight over shoulder guards, a football in his hands. He read the list of names; fourth from the left was Sam Lockhart, the varsity's co-captain.

He had heard of Sam Lockhart. He had read about him in *Ebony*. Lockhart was now playing football at Michigan, and they said he would be All-American. So this was Lockhart's high school.

David pulled himself a little straighter. He would like it here, and perhaps he, too, would play football.

He moved on down the hall until he saw a door with a brass plate marked Office and joined a line of students waiting there. School had started three weeks ago in North Town, and David gathered from the conversations going on around him that most of those waiting wanted to make changes in their programs. He hoped he was not in the wrong line, but he asked no questions.

"I got old Peterson again for English," the boy ahead of him was saying to a girl whose curly blonde ponytail was tied with a bright red ribbon.

"I had her last year," the girl exclaimed, "and was she ever a tight marker! All she cares about is description and she loves to give 50's. She won't ever give anybody over 89—says the kids don't do half enough in her course."

David thought that they sounded just like the boys and girls he had gone to school with in South Town. Only it was funny the way they pronounced their words, especially those with r sounds—year and her and course. He pursed his lips to imitate the sound, but when he silently repeated the words, they were not the same.

"Course," he said again, aloud, but he knew that his r was muted.

The boy ahead turned. "Did you get Peterson?" he asked.

David was embarrassed. "No, I don't know," he tried to explain. "I didn't get anybody yet."

"You must be new. Are you a freshie?"

"Yes—Well, not exactly. I'm new here, but I've already been to high school."

"Where you from? Detroit?"

"No. I went to Pocohantas County Training School. I just—My folks just came to North Town."

"Never heard of Pocohantas County. Whereabouts is that?"

"It's down South."

"Oh, say! Were you on television in those sit-in strikes? I saw a lot of those pictures."

The line moved forward before David could reply. Perhaps it was just as well, he thought.

"You play football?" the boy continued. David nodded. "We had a colored fellow here last year as half-back, made all-state. He graduated. Now we got Buck Taylor. Do you know him?"

David shook his head. No, he had not heard of him.

"What kind of team did they have at your school?" the girl asked with interest.

"We didn't play football so much at home," David answered. He wished now that they had. "We played baseball and basketball mostly."

"Well, say, you ought to go out for football anyway," the boy suggested. "You got size now, and you ought to be fast." He went on to describe the past successes of Central High's football team.

David found himself surprised at how easy it was to talk to him.

"What year are you?" asked the girl.

"I'm supposed to be a senior."

"Yeah, but they put you back when you transfer," she announced. "They always do that. Like no other school could be as good as ours."

David took a deep breath and looked around. Inside he felt funny. He was entering a high school in the North, and while it was not a "colored" school, it was not a "white" school either. Here he was, talking with white people who did not treat him as inferior or as anything special. He had never before talked with anyone white this way—just as students together, friendly and equal. But, he told himself, this boy and this girl were probably unusual. He must not be foolish. There were those who had nearly knocked him down a little while ago.

The line moved forward again, and the girl passed through the door. David could see people inside the office checking records, looking up information in file cabinets, and marking the students' course cards.

When it was his turn, a girl who looked like a student glanced at his report card from Pocohantas County

Training School and, after a few questions, sent him with another card to a counselor in an inner office.

Until now, David had not realized how many courses a school in the North offered and what a wide range of choices students had. At his school in the South, everyone in the same class had to take the same subjects, and almost all of them were taught by the same teacher. His principal had prepared a typed statement describing his work and the studies at the Training School. The counselor now studied it carefully, and although David told him he hoped to go to college after high school, the counselor enrolled him in the vocational course, rather than the college preparatory. Later, he said, David might make a change. He classified him as a sophomore.

His first day so many things were new that at times David was confused, but he still hesitated to ask questions. He wanted to talk with some of the colored boys he saw, but each one seemed busy with his own affairs. With the white students he was even more uncertain. Fearing he might be rebuffed or considered forward, he was very unsure of his place.

At lunchtime he lingered outside the door of the school cafeteria until he saw another colored student approaching. The boy was almost as tall as David but heavier, wider in the shoulders, and he was lighter in color. He and the redheaded fellow with him wore white pullovers with red C's on them.

David followed them into the cafeteria and, watching carefully, did just what the colored fellow did, even to selecting the same food for his lunch. After paying the cashier, he sat down at the same table with his guide, who looked at him for the first time. His look did not make David feel welcome, and he did not respond when David said, "Hi!"

The redhead, on the other hand, seemed less annoyed than startled. "Are you a freshie?" he asked.

"Well, I'm new," David answered. "I transferred."

"So you didn't know, huh! Didn't anybody tell you that freshies and new men don't eat in here?"

David looked at the colored student, who made no response. "No," he said, "nobody told me."

"Well, that's the way it is, but since you have your tray, you can take it with you. You'll have to go to the fire basement. You go out that door and go down the hall. Halfway there's a red button marked Fire, and you push that, and when the elevator comes, you go down to the fire basement with the other new boys and freshmen."

So there was a special place for new people, David realized. It was with the freshmen in the basement, probably next to the boiler room. They were not sending him away because he was colored. He smiled to show that he was not angry. As he walked toward the door, he noticed two tables full of colored students and wished he had seen them before.

Halfway down the hall, just as he had been told, he saw the button. Balancing his tray in his left hand, he pushed.

Instantly it seemed that all the fire sirens in the world had gone off.

Doors flew open, but in no door was there anything like an elevator. Within seconds, the hall had filled with people. It was a fire drill.

The two sweater wearers were suddenly on each side of David; the white boy took his tray from him and laid it on a radiator. Laughing, they each took him by an arm and hurried him down the stairway and out to the street. They had thought he would know better and they were sorry, they said; but they still laughed.

For the rest of the day David was less interested in what he was doing than in what might result from his awful blunder.

When he got home that afternoon his mother and his sister, Betty Jane, were anxious to hear about his first day at the new school. He poured himself a glass of milk, took a handful of cookies from the cooky jar, and sat down at the kitchen table opposite them. After talking some about his classes, he tried to describe the huge gymnasium, the well-equipped shops, and the science room with its gleaming modern laboratory. When his mother asked him about the other colored students, he told her that he had spoken to one, but he did not say that his greeting had not been returned.

It had been Betty Jane's first day at school, too, and she was full of enthusiasm.

"I don't mind getting put back," she said. "I'm still no older than most of the kids in fifth grade. Besides if I was in sixth grade, I might have had one of the meanest teachers in the whole school. As it is, I got one of the best."

David was tall and dark like his father, but Betty Jane

was like her mother. She was lighter than David, and her hair was sleek and glossy like an Indian's. Mrs. Williams was just medium height, and Betty Jane was still small for her ten years.

Before she married, Mrs. Williams had taught in a two-room school. She had had more formal education than her husband, but he knew more about city life for he had worked on factory jobs in Southern cities before coming North.

"My school has a gym, too," Betty Jane hurried on. "And a cooking room for the girls. And guess what? A library with just hundreds and thousands of books. And I can bring them home and don't have to pay. Nobody at home in South Town could ever imagine such a school," she concluded in a burst of enthusiasm.

Mrs. Williams laughed and kissed her.

"How did you get along with the others?" she asked. "You know, the white children?"

"Oh, they were all right," Betty Jane replied quickly. "Tenth Street School is mostly colored. We have some colored teachers, too, but they're just like the others and nobody pays any mind. That is—" Betty Jane paused. "That is mostly nobody pays any mind, but it looks like going to school and coming home the colored kids all walk together and the white kids walk together."

The Williamses were living temporarily in a four-room flat in a dingy two-story building. It was the last in a row of identical frame houses, all of which badly needed a coat of paint. Farther out on Sixth Street, on the east side of North Town, colored people owned comfortable one-

and two-family houses, and Mr. Williams hoped some day to be able to buy one for his family. They had lived in their own house on their own land down South, and apartment-living seemed crowded. However, the flat had been freshly painted, and, after their furniture was installed, they found the place livable.

They had never had a bathroom before, and Mrs. Williams particularly enjoyed the kitchen with its running water and white enameled sink. David was glad he didn't have to carry water from a pump in the backyard, as he had at home. However, he no longer had a room of his own. His room in South Town had been small, but it had been his own. Here he had to sleep on a couch in the living room and to double up with Betty Jane on the closet for his clothes.

The Williamses were on the first floor; another family lived across the hall, and two more on the second floor. The Williamses thought it might be nice to have neighbors so close, but they missed not having a porch and a yard.

David also missed feeding the hens, the pigs, and the cow and gathering the eggs and doing the milking and the other country chores he'd done down South. He missed them, but he was glad to be free. City life, up North, looked good.

When his father came home from work and the family was eating dinner, David jokingly told about his misadventure with the fire alarm. He laughed, but his father did not think it was funny at all.

"Didn't anybody ask who rang the bell?" he asked. "Didn't your principal say anything?"

"No, sir," David said. "After it was over, the fellows said they thought I would know better. They were all right, I guess. I found out afterwards the colored fellow's name is Bruce Taylor, but they call him Buck. He's a senior, and he plays football. The white boy is Mike O'Connor, and he's the captain of the football team."

"I do hope, David," Mrs. Williams cautioned, "that you won't be getting into any trouble. As a new student you've got to be extra careful. Try to get started right."

"Yes, and being colored, too," his father added. "They'll be watching you extra hard, colored and a new-comer from the South."

David reminded himself silently that he would be watching, too. He had said nothing about having been pushed that morning, but he had not forgotten. He would be watching, and if they came at him again, he would be ready.

TWO

THE NEXT MORNING ON DAVID'S WAY TO SCHOOL, two colored boys left the group of friends they were walking with and crossed the street to greet him. Jimmy Hines and Alonzo Wells were their names. It was an act of friendship that David welcomed. They asked David where he was from and how he was classified. Later, in front of the school, Alonzo introduced him to the other members of the group.

"We saw you in the lunchroom yesterday," one of the boys said. "Figured maybe you was a friend of that Buck Taylor."

David said he hadn't known Buck before.

"Buck thinks he's so big," the boy continued.

"Our crowd don't run after the white kids," Jimmy Hines explained. "We know we're just as good as they are—

better than lots of them—because they're treacherous—smile in your face and laugh at you behind your back. We figure to leave them alone, man."

"Oh, Jimmy," one of the girls protested, "you're always talking down the white kids!"

"I'm just trying to let our new friend know what the score is," Jimmy defended himself. "He's just come from down South, probably thinks up North we got the race problem solved—Well, I want him to know what's coming. These paddies going to be down on you, man. You got to watch it!"

Some of the students left, but four or five others chimed in, agreeing with Jimmy. The white people, practically all of them, teachers as well as students, they insisted to David, would try to make life hard for him. He would be given lower grades and fewer chances. They would try to make him look inferior. He wouldn't have a fair chance to make a team, and if he was so good that he had to be put on one, they would still try to make him look bad. The only thing for him to do was to stick with "our crowd."

"They don't bother none of us," one of the boys told him. "They know we're ready, and we don't take no stuff."

David had little time to think about what he had been told. He had to hurry to reach his homeroom before the final bell rang, and then everyone left immediately for an all-school assembly. It was very much like other assemblies he had seen. David was seated at the back of the auditorium, and they all rose to sing "The Star-Spangled Banner" and salute the flag. Then they were seated, and Mr. Hart, the principal, spoke, his words coming out loud and clear over the amplifiers in the big room. He made a few announcements, and there was general laughter when he said that he hoped everybody was now fully recovered from the effects of vacation.

"Yesterday," Mr. Hart began, "yesterday during the lunch period someone set off the fire alarm. We are happy that our building is fireproof, and we are proud of the discipline and good order shown by the faculty and student body in promptly emptying the building, but we cannot allow such potentially dangerous jokes."

He went on to describe the possibility of accidents, the inevitable disruption of programs, and the evils of undisciplined action.

"I want the student, whoever he or she is," he concluded relentlessly, "to stand now so that all of us here can know where the responsibility lies."

Heads turned, and there were murmurs of curiosity, but no one stood.

David was positive that others knew of his guilt. Mike O'Connor and Buck Taylor, the two responsible for his action, would certainly not have kept the story to themselves. To stand up before the whole school seemed impossible. Now they would stare. Afterward they would point him out. They would identify him as the bad colored boy, a newcomer from down South, ignorant and stupid. A lump rose in his throat. He would be expelled. His mother would be ashamed of him. His father would be disappointed and angry. But they already knew, and it was too late now.

He pushed himself to his feet. "I did it, sir," he said in a voice so low and husky that only those close by heard him.

Around him, a sea of white faces turned to look. David's eyes were blurred, but he knew they were staring at him. He heard a buzz of talk and the sound of laughter. Then he heard the principal's voice over the public-address system saying that he should report to the office after assembly. He sank into his seat utterly miserable. At last the assembly was dismissed, and he was free to leave the auditorium.

David waited in the principal's outer office. His dejection was so deep that he didn't look up until someone stood right in front of him.

"Hey, fellow," Mike O'Connor greeted him with a big smile. "It took guts to stand up and take it like that, but you didn't have to do it. I was going to tell old Hart myself—later—not naming any names."

David did not answer. "But I'll tell him now," Mike volunteered. "He'll understand. Everything'll be all right."

After Mr. Hart had led both boys into his private office, Mike told him the whole story, taking all the blame. He talked as though he knew no one would be punished. He said it was just a joke that had gone too far.

But Mr. Hart did not smile. Finally he dismissed Mike, telling him he would send for him again.

The principal seated himself behind his desk and told David to take a chair. He wanted to know David's name and then asked about his earlier schooling. David tried to answer all the questions.

"We had all the grades," he said, "from first grade on

up through high school. They had other elementary schools in the county, but ours was the only high school— I mean, for colored."

Mr. Hart seemed pleased when he learned that David hoped to go through college and medical school and become a doctor.

"That was one reason," David explained, "that my folks wanted to come North, so I could get better schooling."

There were more questions about his family. David was polite, but he made his answers short and was careful about what he said. He might have said that his family had been caught in the storm of hate and violence that was sweeping over his native state, that in his own hometown, just a few weeks ago a white friend of theirs had been killed by a sudden volley of gunfire from night-riding men. He might have told him that as a result they had been jailed, all of them, even his little sister, and that his father had been so badly beaten in jail that he still was not completely well. However, although these things were very much in David's mind, he said nothing about them.

"Why did your father decide to live in North Town?" Mr. Hart asked.

"Well, I guess he didn't decide that at first," David answered. "We were supposed to drive to Detroit, but we stopped here overnight with some friends who used to live near us at home, and they said this was a better place to live than any of the big cities, better for work and better for schooling. And this friend, Mr. Crutchfield, said he could help my father get a job where he worked. My father had his trade, and the next day he got hired right away at the Foundation Iron and Machine Works."

A bell was ringing. The principal stood, ending the conference.

"David," he said with kindness, "you might have trouble getting adjusted. Let me know if I can help. I don't mean for every little thing—somebody might call you a dirty name, and you may think you're getting pushed around some—but if there is anything important, just walk in the door and tell them out front you have an appointment with me. I'll see you."

Even the principal seemed to feel there would be trouble.

THREE

David did not tell his parents what Jimmy Hines had said about the unfair treatment at Central. First of all, he didn't believe all of it, and anyway, he decided, it was up to him to keep his eyes open and make up his own mind.

The next day in the general science lab, one of the colored boys he had met asked him a question about an experiment they were doing.

"I don't think I've got it figured out," David replied. "I missed the first month, and I've got to do a lot of extra work to catch up."

"Aw, there's nothing to this," the boy bragged. "I had all this stuff before in grade school. I even flunked it last year 'cause I never turned in no notebook."

"But I never had science before," David explained, "not like this anyway, not in a real laboratory. I'll have to study."

"It don't mean nothing to me, man. Besides, I'm going in the Air Force next year. I'll get my science there."

The two got acquainted, and the boy invited David to join his friends at noon for lunch. They turned out to be the same group of colored students David had noticed on his first day in the cafeteria, and they were friends of Jimmy's and Alonzo's. No one had told them to eat in one place, and they knew they were not being segregated. It was rather that they chose to keep together. They seemed to be more comfortable that way. David found himself enjoying their company for they made him welcome. They laughed a great deal. They laughed loud, and they talked loud. They seemed to be trying to show they were not afraid.

The conversation turned to football, and David couldn't help asking Jimmy Hines, who had joined the group, how Sam Lockhart got to be co-captain of the team. "He was colored," David said.

"Yeah, old Sam made it," Jimmy admitted, "but you don't know how it is. It's one of two things: You got to be twice as good, or else you got to play Uncle Tom. Now you take our boy, Lonzo Wells. He's good, better than that Buck Taylor, but Lonzo don't take nothing off of nobody."

An argument developed about Alonzo, and whether or not he was always looking for trouble. David said nothing, but he decided in his own mind that he was going to succeed at Central. Others had done it, and he believed that he could, too.

For physical education in the gymnasium that afternoon, David took off his leather-heeled shoes and stripped to the waist. He had no gym shoes or gym uniform yet. With the other boys he performed some calisthenics, and then he was made part of a squad with a student leader. He was awkward and self-conscious on the parallel bars and rings because he had never used them before. Some of the fellows laughed at him. He laughed, too, to cover his embarrassment.

After class was dismissed, the instructor beckoned him into the office that opened directly off the gym floor.

"Ever do any apparatus work before?" the instructor asked, and when David was slow to answer, he added, "Do you know the shoulder roll or the flying Dutchman?"

"No, sir, I've never heard of anything like that," David said.

"You new here? Where did you go to school before?"

David told him it was in the South—in the country, really—and they did not have a gym there.

"Have you played any football?" the instructor asked.

"Well, sir, I played. But our school was small, and we didn't have a real good team like you all."

The instructor encouraged David to try for the squad; and as a result, a few days later, David reported to the team locker room and was issued football equipment.

However, the only gear that was left so late in the season was in poor shape, held together with extra cords and lacings. When Alonzo Wells saw David struggling with it, he crossed the room to offer him a hand.

"They shouldn't give you this crap," he complained. "Hey, manager!" he shouted. "You got two left shoulder guards here, and both of them busted. What you expect this new man to do?"

"Tell him to keep driving to the left, Alonzo," someone joked.

Mike O'Connor looked up from the bench, where he was putting on his shoes. "Hi there, Fire Chief," he said, smiling. "Get your signals straight out there!"

The freckle-faced team manager tried unsuccessfully to lace the two left shoulder guards together, and then agreed that David would have to get along without them.

David's helmet fitted badly and the front was broken, but just the same he felt pretty good as he ran out to the field with enough other fellows in uniform to make four or five teams. He jogged around the cinder track with Alonzo, trying to look like one of the regulars and wondering how they ran so well with all their gear and with heavy cleats weighing down their feet. Buck Taylor loped easily past them, but he did not turn his head.

"You tired?" Alonzo asked, puffing, as they neared the end of the second lap.

"Not much," David said shortly, though he really was.

"Supposed to make this five times around."

Five times! David knew he could never do it.

He ran on, not talking, trying to save his wind. Alonzo pulled ahead. Halfway round again, David's heart was pounding hard. He slowed still more, wanting at least to get back to the starting point, but before he could finish the third lap, he gave out and dropped panting on the turf. He lay on his back, his eyes closed, his wind coming in hard gasps.

"Can't you make it?" Alonzo asked a little while later. "The man don't want you to rest too long. He'll tell you to keep going. Course, I know how it is, first time out. Still it's better to keep going."

David pushed himself to his feet; he had his wind back. Some of the others, having already completed their laps, were walking in tight circles or jogging in place. Across the field, under the direction of a coach, players were tackling a dummy suspended on a line. Others, each carrying a football, were diving and rolling. No one was scrimmaging. It all looked like work, hard, steady, driving work, David decided.

Alonzo took his place at the foot of a line practicing passing and receiving, and David fell in opposite him. The ball zigzagged down the line as far as the fellow on David's right. Instead of passing it to Alonzo, who would have thrown it across to David, he quickly shot the ball back up to the top of the line again. Once more the ball worked its way down.

"Kirinski, here!" Alonzo called out.

But again Kirinski fired the ball to the other end. Then he turned with a look of mock surprise on his face. "You call me, Lonzo? What you want?"

"I don't want no mess. That's what I don't want."

"Man, neither do I," Kirinski said. "I sure don't want no mess."

Somebody up the line cautioned, "Watch it, Kirinski!"

The ball came down the line. At the very instant that it started toward Kirinski, Alonzo leaped forward. He and Kirinski collided, and they both went down.

"Bastard," Alonzo shouted. "Stinking Polack bastard!"

A whistle blew. Some of the boys helped Kirinski to his feet.

"You didn't have to do that," one of them said angrily to Alonzo.

"Just who do you think you are?" another demanded.

David stood rooted in place, wondering what he should do.

"I told you no tackling," said the coach, pushing his way through the crowd. "You there!" He pointed at Alonzo. "Get off the field! You might as well turn in your uniform. We can't use people like you at Central."

"I only showed him," Alonzo argued, defiant. "He was playing tricks, and I showed him."

"I'm the coach here. I'll do the showing and I know all the tricks. You get off the field!" He watched suspiciously as Alonzo turned and started away. "And if anybody don't like it," he added, looking directly at David, "he can go along with you."

David wanted very much to go, to leave with his friend, but he also wanted very much to stay.

Kirinski was saying that he was O.K., that he didn't know why the crazy joker had jumped him like that.

The coach was still looking at David. "All right!" he

said. "I guess you want to go along with your buddy. So get going, huh!"

Yes, he certainly would go along with his buddy. David turned; walking with what dignity he could command, he left the field. He was angry. He was angry with the whole crowd; he was angry with the coach who had asked no questions but just assumed that the colored player was the one at fault; and he was angry with the other players who had failed to defend Alonzo. He was angry, too, at himself because he had not left the field before the coach drove him away.

"Wait, Lonzo," he called and broke into a run. "I'm coming."

FOUR

IN THE LOCKER ROOM AFTER PRACTICE WAS OVER, the coach called the whole squad together.

"All of you know how I feel," he announced. "I don't care what color a man is if he can play football and be a part of a team. If green men from Mars show up and they can make the team, I'll play them. But a team can't hold hotheads who want to show how bad they can be. We threw one man out today. Then his buddy chose to go with him. Well, that's all right with me. Maybe it saves trouble up ahead."

Buck Taylor, who was listening carefully from the back of the locker room, believed that what the coach said was true. He felt that he had always been treated fairly. He knew that he wasn't as good as some of the other players. He was fast—that was his one great talent—but sometimes he fumbled, and often he drew penalties for the team.

The coach had always been fair to him, Buck felt, and Mike O'Connor, the present captain, was one of the finest fellows he had ever known. The rest of the guys—most of them, anyway—had always been O.K. A few had ignored him, and some maybe had tried to be mean, but he had always been able to get along without fighting. He had learned how to do this from his father.

"White people will respect you if you respect yourself," Mr. Taylor said. "Trouble with the colored man is he often wants more than he has earned or more than he deserves. He expects somebody to hand him something. I don't want anybody to hand me anything. I'll go after what I want, and I'll get what's mine."

Buck admired his father's forcefulness, but he was somewhat awed by his father's brains and the stories he told of his early struggles. Born on a farm in Georgia, Mr. Taylor had worked his way through trade school in the South, then married and supported his family as a carpenter. Later, after moving to North Town, he had developed a real-estate business and studied law, finally passing the bar examination.

Buck believed that other colored men could have done what his father had done if they had only tried, but he also believed that he was quite different from other colored boys of his age. Being a football player helped to support his feeling of superiority. He knew that most of the other colored students didn't like him, but he didn't care. He had a small group of close friends. Jeanette

Lenoir, whose family was from New Orleans, was one of them. Jeanette's father, a postal clerk, had been transferred North two years ago. Through Mr. Taylor's real-estate office, he had bought a comfortable house on the west side, two blocks from Buck's home.

"Paid spot cash for it, too," Mr. Taylor often said when he pointed out the Lenoir home to his prospects.

During football season, Buck kept training rules—in the house by nine every night and in bed by ten. However, he didn't always go right to sleep, and that night he felt like telling Jeanette what had happened that afternoon on the football field. He brought the phone into his room, and shut the door on the long cord. Sitting cross-legged on his bed, his bare chest showing dark against his blue pajama jacket, he dialed her number.

After listening to the story, Jeanette wanted to know more about the background of David Williams.

Buck was sure that he had David all figured out, and he told her so. "The first day I saw him I said to myself, Another one of them scared spooks from down behind the sun, ignorant and dumb."

He listened, frowning, then he went on.

"I've told you before, even if you and your folks did come from the South—well, mine did, too, as far as that's concerned—that these down South farm people are really trouble. First, they're so scared they can't do anything for themselves. Then they think they know so much nobody can do anything with them."

Buck swung his feet over the edge of the bed and stood up.

"You take what happened today," he argued. "This guy Wells jumps bad, and he deserved what he got. He asked for it. Probably this new boy put him up to it—Yes, they were working together—and Kirinski is a good guy, you know. He's all right—Hunh?—No. What is there to say? —No I don't mean to ask Wells or this guy Williams anything. I don't have anything to say to them—Because they don't have anything to say to me—They'll be griping. White folks don't give you a chance, white folks down on us poor colored folks—Yeah—Well now you know as well as I do . . ."

He was silent for a while.

"Look, Jeanette, now look," he said, interrupting her. "You know I'm as sorry as anybody for those people over in the flats, but my dad's got plenty of houses that they can buy if they really want to get out of the slums. They like it, I tell you. My dad says the same thing, and if they move out into a nice neighborhood, they bring the rest of the lot right along with them—Well, I know, but you're the exception."

He scowled.

"No!" He was short with her. "No, I'm not going to ask David Williams anything—Well, I hope you won't—First thing you know he'll be wanting to date you—No, you wouldn't—No, you wouldn't, for one thing your old man wouldn't let you—Listen, Jeanette, if you do ask him, if you carry it that far, you know what'll happen to you with all the bunch of decent guys? They'll drop you like a hot potato. Yes—and maybe I do mean that—What?—Jeanette? Jeanette?"

He took the receiver from his ear and looked at it with a frown. It only buzzed.

The next morning, after he reached school, Buck waited for Jeanette at her locker. Some of his friends, who knew that he liked her, saw him standing there and smiled. They thought that Buck and Jeanette made an attractive pair. He watched as she hurried up the hall in a bright yellow rain cape and hood, her steps firm and quick. Her smile was warm and friendly as though she had not hung up on their conversation. As she shrugged out of her wraps and dug into the locker for a book, she spoke of her need to hurry.

"I'll see you later," he said abruptly. Without waiting for a reply, he turned and walked away.

Jeanette, with an armload of books, made her way to science class. She saw David going in the door ahead of her, as she stopped to greet her friend Maybelle Reed. Of the two, Maybelle was the one everyone noticed first. She was very pretty with light brown skin, naturally straight hair, and a pleasant, easy smile.

Jeanette was tall for a girl, and slim. In color she was as dark as David. She had large eyes and highly arched eyebrows, which gave to her face a questioning look. She smiled often, but she seemed also to be thoughtful and serious, and she walked as though she knew where she was going and what she would do when she arrived.

This morning at the end of the class period she waved at David to indicate that she wanted him to wait for her. She left Maybelle and walked across the room, meeting him as they both neared toward the door.

"You seem to like this study about plants and pollination," she said.

"Well, it's kind of interesting, I guess." He tried to seem casual. "I've seen it working before, but I never did know what was going on, not really."

"Your father wasn't a farmer, was he?"

"Well, he wasn't much of a farmer, and while we didn't do any cross-pollination, they had it on the big farms, and I always wondered about it. Seems funny," he went on, "to be studying about growing things and fertilizing and pollinizing up here in a big city high school."

"Yes," Jeanette agreed, "lots of things seem funny. We've only been here for about two years. I know what you mean."

They moved down the hall, not saying much. At the end of the hall, she turned toward the stairs.

"I have first lunch period," he said hastily.

"So do I," Jeanette answered.

"How about—" He stopped. "How about meeting you—"

"Yes, I'd love to." Jeanette was smiling. "We could meet right here and maybe go over to the Nut House. I like hamburgers."

Later, while they ate in the crowded confusion of the lunchroom across the street, David found himself telling Jeanette all about Alonzo and the football coach.

"I know how white folks are," he concluded. "I learned about them down South, but I'm going to get my schooling just the same. Only I'd like to get the chance to try like anybody else. I don't want any special favors. I just don't want white people holding me back all my life."

He wondered afterward if Jeanette agreed with him. She did not say.

In the locker room that afternoon as the players were dressing for football practice, Mike O'Connor said to Buck, "You know I've been thinking about that guy Williams. Thought I'd try to talk to him, but he wasn't in the cafeteria today."

"I don't know what there is to talk about," Buck said, not trying to hide his annoyance. "He had his chance just like anybody else. Nobody did anything to him."

"I know. Just the same maybe he thinks somebody did. He's from the country, you know."

"Lots of guys are from the country."

"Why don't you try to talk to him, Buck? Maybe you could help him."

"Who, me?" Buck was really angry now. "Why should I? He's not my baby. He's nothing to me, less than nothing."

"O.K., O.K." Mike watched while Buck stamped into a shoe and bent to lace it with swift hard motions. "You don't have to bust a gut about it."

FIVE

Getting up Sunday mornings without having a regular round of duties was another thing that made David realize that his new life was very different from his old. He had grown up knowing that regardless of the day or the weather, good times or bad, sickness or even death, the livestock had to be fed and the cow milked. He had been taught the Ten Commandments, and he could recite the one about the Sabbath by heart: "In it thou shalt not do any work, thou, nor thy son, nor thy daughter, thy manservant, nor thy maidservant, nor thy cattle, nor thy stranger that is within thy gates." But down South he had never heard anyone preach against doing the necessary farm chores.

"Seems funny not to have to worry about feeding and milking and cutting firewood and all that," David said at the breakfast table on Sunday morning.

"It's all just what you get used to," his father replied. "I guess we couldn't go back to wood stoves if we wanted to. Right, Dave? And where would we find the wood?"

"One thing," Mrs. Williams said, a wistful look coming over her face, "we didn't have to pay for fuel, and we always had eggs and most of the time vegetables out of the garden."

"I guess you do miss the things around home," Mr. Williams admitted.

"It's more the people," Mrs. Williams tried to explain. "It looks like we don't have friends here. We don't know people. We don't really even know the people who share this house with us. Yes, I miss my friends."

"How about the Crutchfields?" David reminded his mother. "They're real friends now, and after they take us to church today, you'll be making a lot more new friends."

"They'll be wanting you to teach Sunday school as soon as they get to know you." Betty Jane remembered with pride how the students and older people, too, had admired her mother's teaching. "You must have been a good teacher, Ma. I wish I could have been in your school."

"You're right, Betty Jane." Mr. Williams leaned back in his chair, smiling. "Your mother was one of the best, and she could still do it."

"Your father's a little biased in my favor." Mrs. Williams was laughing, but David could see she was pleased, as she got up and started clearing the table. "We've got to get a move on. The Crutchfields will be here soon to pick us up, and we don't want to keep them waiting. Ed, you'll go with us, won't you?"

Mr. Williams shook his head slowly. "Honey, you and the children go along. Maybe I'll get a sermon on TV," he said.

"Is your head hurting?" David asked.

"Not just now. It's not bad, but when I sit still, like in church, then it gets worse."

"Ed, I want you to see a doctor." David had often heard his mother say the same thing before, but today she sounded particularly anxious.

"Nothing for a doctor to do." Mr. Williams shrugged and spread his hands wide on the table. "He'd give me some aspirin or something, or he'd tell me I need a rest. Might tell me to get a change of climate, go South, take a trip to Florida. Yeah!" he elaborated as he saw the smiles around him. "That's just about all I need, a nice trip South."

All of them tried to laugh, but David could see in his father's eyes the look of deep pain mixed with anger and bitterness. David knew that he was remembering the horror of those days before they had moved when, because he had defied a white man, he had been jailed and beaten and his family had been terrorized by a mob. Now they tried not to think about what had happened, but they could not forget it. The subject was never openly discussed, and they did not talk about how they felt. When anyone mentioned the matter at all, it was referred to as "the trouble," and everyone knew what was meant. They spoke of events "before the trouble" or "after the trouble."

As the family started to dress in their Sunday clothes, Mr. Williams caught some of their enthusiasm, in spite of his headache, and decided he would come with them after all.

"Can't have my family going out to meet the public like they didn't have a daddy in the house," he said.

Betty Jane was watching at the front window when the Crutchfields drove up. She waved and ran to the door. Everyone was ready to leave except David who complained that he was always the last one to get into the bathroom.

Mr. Crutchfield was standing beside his car when the Williams family reached the sidewalk. He held the door open for them like a servant proud of his employers.

"My, my!" He bowed and smiled broadly. "Don't you all ladies look fine this morning! Don't know when my old hack has hauled such beautiful ladies and such well-set-up gentlemen."

They exchanged pleasantries, and the Williamses piled into the back seat.

"Don't mind Andy," Mrs. Crutchfield said. "He goes on like that all the time."

"Course," Andy Crutchfield retorted, as he settled his large body behind the wheel, "you all know that this fine lady sitting up here beside me is my real boss. Like the man said, I the one drive the car but she the one drive me."

Andy Crutchfield had left South Town many years ago, and was now firmly established in North Town. Without skills or special training, he had found work at the Foundation Iron and Machine Works as a janitor. For seventeen years, he had survived layoffs and cutbacks, boasting that he never missed a day except at vacation time, which was always spent among his old friends in the South. Like the Williamses, many families making their way northward had stopped overnight at the Crutchfield home.

As they entered the church, people in the vestibule greeted the Crutchfields as friends. An usher, wearing white gloves, led them down the center aisle to a pew near the front. The service of worship had not yet started. David sat very straight and tried to look as though he had been there before. Betty Jane, openly curious, turned and twisted in her seat. She peered at the painted angels and cherubs on the ceiling and studied the leaded patterns of the stained-glass windows.

The organist played a few bars softly and then started a hymn. The voices of the choir members sounded melodiously from the back of the church. From the pew behind them, someone passed an open hymnbook to Mrs. Williams. David reached for a book in the rack and found his place.

It was a song that David had liked to sing at home. Now it seemed quite grand with the pipe organ and a large choir of good voices.

"Holy, Holy, Holy!" they sang, "Lord God almighty! Early in the morning our song shall rise to Thee." At the start of the second verse everyone stood up and the choir began to file, two by two, down the center aisle. "Holy, Holy, Holy! All the saints adore Thee." The singers, like the organist, were robed in dark red. As they passed, David clearly heard the sopranos, *"Cherubim and seraphim, falling down before Thee"*; the altos, *"Who wert and art, and evermore shall be"*; the tenors, *"All Thy works shall praise Thy name in earth and sky and sea"*; and the basses whose voices seemed to rumble and growl, *"Holy, Holy, Holy, Merciful and Mighty."*

At the front of the sanctuary the procession divided with practiced smoothness, one line going to the right and the other to the left to take their places in the choir sections. When the last verse came to an end, the minister walked to the pulpit. He quoted one passage of Scripture, and the congregation responded with another.

"The Lord is in His Holy temple: let all the earth keep silence before Him."

The minister bowed his head and quietly said a short prayer. It was as though he knew that God was there and it was not necessary to shout to get His attention. As he concluded the prayer, many joined in saying, "Amen."

David knew that some of the worshipers, perhaps most of them, had once lived in the South. They were Negroes who had decided that "going North" would mean better opportunities to earn a living and to educate their children. Some, like the Crutchfields, had come North many years ago. Others, David guessed, were probably newcomers like himself. He imagined that most of them had more education than the people left in South Town, more money, too. They earned more and they lived better.

The sermon was also different—there was much more about citizenship and voting than in the sermons David was used to. The Reverend Mr. Hayes, who was over six feet tall and very thin, had bushy white hair, which stood out from his head. At first, he preached about Moses and the children of Israel. David knew the story well, but this time the minister had taken his text from a less familiar part. It told how the people complained after Moses had led them out of the land of Egypt. Once he freed them of their bondage to Pharaoh, they blamed everything that went wrong on Moses.

Probably no one in the church was old enough to have been a slave, but they had all heard stories of that time. They often sang songs that came down from slave days and heard preachers compare the Bible stories of slavery in Egypt with the history of slavery in America.

The Reverend Mr. Hayes was saying that the lesson to be learned from the Bible story did not apply only to the physical slavery of the past. It applied as well to people here and now. He talked about the slavery of poverty and unemployment and contrasted it to industrial prosperity. Then he compared the slavery of ignorance with the liberty of knowledge and understanding. There were many, he said, who complained when they achieved freedom and opportunity because they then had to meet greater responsibilities.

Among the responsibilities all must meet, he claimed, was that of citizenship. An election was pending, and campaign speeches were blaring forth from radio and television sets. The Reverend Mr. Hayes told the congregation that voting was more than a right and a privilege. It was a duty, and every citizen had a responsibility to consider the candidates and to examine the issues and then to vote for good government.

"Our prophets," he said, "Frederick Douglass, Booker T. Washington, and W. E. B. DuBois cried out, 'Let my people go!' We have come out of the land of bondage. We are called to new tasks and new responsibilities, in conduct and industry, in thrift and education, in citizenship and brotherhood. Many of us in North Town today are complaining like those lost children in the wilderness, complaining and refusing to use what we have to make life better, complaining about what our leaders do not give us, what our politicians will not do for us, never thinking how much we can and should do for ourselves."

After church the Crutchfields joined the Williams family for dinner. They talked enthusiastically about the sermon and the church program. Andy Crutchfield was loud in praise of his pastor, and Mrs. Crutchfield applauded the missionary society's work, caring for the needy at home and raising money for churches in Africa.

"How long does a man have to be in North Town before he can vote?" Mr. Williams asked.

"I don't know," Andy Crutchfield said. "I don't mess with politics. Never voted yet, and don't aim to. That's one thing I don't go along with Reverend Hayes on. Voting! Only place I vote is in church meeting. I vote there, and I know what I'm voting on."

"Down South, they didn't let us vote," Mr. Williams said. "I always figured that if they ever would allow it in my county I'd want to be among the first to walk in there and express myself."

"What difference you suppose your one little vote is going to make?"

"Might not make much difference to anybody else, but voting in a public election, whenever I get the chance, is sure going to make a big difference to me." Mr. Williams pushed his chair back from the table and stood up. "I'm going to say: Here I come, me, Edward Mansfield Williams! I'm voting as a free-born citizen. It won't be anything more than others are doing, but it will be the first time for me, and when I vote, then I'll know I've got some real equality, 'cause my one vote will weigh as much as any other man's, be he high as a Georgia pine or white as new cotton."

SIX

IN NOVEMBER, AT THE END OF THE FIRST MARKING PERIOD, David was again called to the principal's office. This time Mr. Hart was smiling as he greeted him. He glanced at a paper on his desk and remarked that David had made some good grades.

"At our last meeting you told me something about your parents, David," he said. "How are they getting along? Are they settled yet?"

"Not really," David replied. "They're still looking for a better place to live," he explained. "We'd like to buy a house."

"Is your father still working at the Foundation plant?"

"Yes," David said, adding that they had joined the First Baptist Church and made some friends there.

"How do you like Central?" Mr. Hart was persistent.

David hesitated. "I like it very well, sir," he said after a moment's thought.

"I know it still seems new," Mr. Hart said. "And I don't pretend to know how you feel about us," he continued, "but I'm sure there've been problems in getting adjusted. Do you think you've adjusted to us? To the school in general?"

"I guess so." David was noncommittal.

"Have you made many friends? Close friends, I mean?"

"No," David answered, "not really. Not like I used to have."

"Have you been out for any sports? You look like good football material."

For a minute David wanted to tell Mr. Hart what had happened that day on the football field.

"Yes, sir. I went out one day," he said slowly. "I guess I didn't do much."

"Well, the basketball season is coming up. Maybe you'll want to try for that team."

David did not look at the principal. "I don't think I will," he murmured.

After he had gone to bed that night, David thought of some of the things he should have said in answer to Mr. Hart's questions.

Problems in getting adjusted? Yes! Why couldn't he, David Andrew Williams, age sixteen, be recognized as a student who was a human being, just like any other at North Central?

In his classes he was proving that he could do the work. In geometry he did better than most of the white students. In science and in English, he kept up easily. He had been behind in mechanical drawing because he had never before used drafting instruments, but in the machine shop he had caught on fast, and evenings at home he discussed the work with his father who gave him pointers.

One thing about the school, he could not understand. In class, when he recited, he was listened to with interest. In the classrooms and shops the white boys and the girls, too, talked readily with him. They seemed to respect his opinion in discussions. However, in the halls or outside the building everything was different. White boys seldom spoke to him, and they never walked with him or stopped to talk. The white girls were even more distant. When he met one he knew from a class, she often seemed not to recognize him. Sometimes they deliberately looked away, or even worse, they acted as though he were not really there.

He told himself that he did not mind. He knew that there was a book written by a Negro about Negroes called *The Invisible Man*. He knew something about how the invisible man must have felt.

He told himself that he did not mind. But deep inside of him, he did mind. He minded very much. He minded, and he was hurt.

Any friends? The people he knew best at North Central were not his friends. He knew without being told that Alonzo and Jimmy and their crowd were not going anywhere in life. They were not interested in an education. They had no real goals. He did not belong with that unhappy group, although they had befriended him and he spent much of his free time with them.

Jeanette had seemed friendly, but he had not really

talked with her since that day they had had lunch together. She seemed to be always busy with her own affairs and with her own friends like Maybelle Reed and Buck Taylor.

David wished that he could talk to Buck Taylor. Buck excelled as an athlete and as a student, but Buck, like the white students, showed no interest in David.

There were other colored boys who, apparently easy-going and relaxed like Buck, were active in school affairs; but they, too, appeared indifferent to David. Certainly he did not want to be friendly with white people—he did not trust them—but he did not want to be totally ignored by them, either.

If only he could do something important in the school, David thought, then they would know that he was there. If only he had made the football team, or could play the trumpet, or maybe the drums in the band, if only he could do something to make them recognize that he belonged, that he was a person who had something to share. He was looking forward with the best of them to getting an education, and he knew he was capable of doing it.

He should have said all this to the principal, and now he was angry at himself because he had not been able to speak out.

One morning after science class, Jeanette surprised him with an invitation.

"I'd like you to come to Guild meeting at church next Sunday," she told him. "The son of our rector will be the speaker. They say he's very smart. He teaches in one of the church schools in the South."

"I guess I know what he'll be saying," David answered. "I don't have to hear it from anybody else. I could tell them what happened with my family."

"Yes, guess you could." Jeanette was serious. "Most of the people here think that Abraham Hamilton is crazy to be teaching in the South when he could be teaching here."

"I don't. Somebody's got to do it. I figure to go back, after I get my education," David announced firmly.

"That's what I mean. He might need somebody from the South to help him get his point over."

David arrived at St. Cyprian's parish house after the meeting had started and took a seat at the back. Jeanette saw him come in, and she smiled her welcome. He noticed Buck Taylor sitting next to Maybelle Reed, who, with one or two others David knew, turned and nodded in greeting. In the front seats with the older people was the rector, Father Hamilton, in his white clerical collar and black suit.

Mr. Hamilton, the speaker, was describing the poverty and the ignorance in the section of the South where he was principal of a mission school. It seemed there was no public high school for colored children in the county, and very few of the people sent their children to the church school.

"As I stand here speaking to you about our people, I know that it is difficult, if not impossible, for you to realize the conditions there. But I can say that when I stand before an audience there and describe the schools you have and the homes you live in, they do not understand. They cannot believe me. Sometimes they say that not in heaven itself will white children and colored children attend the same schools, study the same books, and work together on the same problems."

He closed with an appeal to young Negroes to prepare themselves to go into the South to teach, or at the very least, to try to understand the problems. With understanding they would find ways of helping. They could share their benefits through the church mission programs and welfare activities. Through political activity, they could bring about legislation for better public education.

There was only light applause as he took his seat. The young woman in charge of the meeting expressed her thanks to the speaker and called for questions. There were none, and the meeting was adjourned.

After the meeting, hot chocolate was served. Jeanette brought a cup to David, and then they both went forward to join the group around Mr. Hamilton.

"I'm from the South myself," a man was saying to the speaker. "When I was a boy things were pretty bad in some places, although they weren't so bad for my parents. They weren't sharecroppers. They were landowners, and my father sent every one of his children off to school. From what you say, they haven't made much progress in your section. What about integration? Aren't the school authorities working on that?"

"Where I am," Hamilton replied, "most of the people have never heard the word, and the authorities have never done anything about it. In the cities, yes, they have done something." He smiled grimly. "In the state capital they have passed new laws, all designed to prevent any action in support of the Supreme Court's decision of 1954."

"Well," Buck Taylor interjected, "it looks like the Southern Negroes really don't want to help themselves. You say yourself that the parents won't send their children to your school. It looks like they don't care."

"Yes, I know what you mean. It does look like the people don't care." The others looked surprised that the speaker had agreed with Buck. "This is what I mean by understanding. Can you understand that in their ignorance, in their poverty, in their lack of vision, these people are without hope? They aren't happy, but they don't know how to improve their conditions. It's hard, often impossible, for them to realize that education might open the way to a better living. In most families, the work of the children in the fields is necessary for survival. If you ride through the country, you'll see that not only men are working in the fields, planting, cultivating, harvesting, and picking cotton, or whatever it might be, but women, too, and children, children six, seven, and eight years old."

"Oh, I can understand that," Buck said easily, "but what I can't understand is why when those people come North they want to go on living like they did down South. They want to live in the slums. They crowd together in places like East Sixth Street. When they go to our schools, they try to make trouble. It looks like even here they don't try to improve themselves."

David was jolted, and found himself disliking Buck Taylor. He could understand very well what Mr. Hamilton was saying. Although his own parents had been landowners, most of his friends' parents had been sharecroppers. He knew how pupils stayed out of school at planting time and at crop time, and how they dropped out for good as soon as they had learned to read and write.

Yes, he knew just what Mr. Hamilton meant and felt that it was brave of him to spend his life working in the South. This was what he himself had always dreamed of doing. After finishing high school, he would go to the state university and then to medical school. Once he became a doctor, he would go back to the South. He would be interested not only in people's physical health but also in what they thought and felt. He would try to help them to understand themselves and to see the possibilities in their lives, to work and sacrifice to get an education and make a better living in the future.

Mr. Hamilton was saying some of the very things that David himself would have said.

"I'm from the South," Jeanette said, plunging into the discussion. "My family moved here from New Orleans, where conditions were not too bad. We had good homes and good schools. There are three colleges for Negroes right in the city."

"Yes." Mr. Hamilton was quick to agree. "You are quite right. Perhaps I did not make myself clear. I was not speaking of all the South. What has happened in New Orleans, in Atlanta and Nashville and Richmond and many other Southern cities shows what can happen. People are making progress in understanding, and now oppression is diminishing. There is growing appreciation for human rights. There is more recognition of worth. It is for this we strive. It is for more light in the dark places that we pray."

"Then I guess," Buck spoke again, "you don't recommend that all those ignorant Southern people come up North and make it harder for us who don't have any problems."

David saw a look of deep sadness come over Mr. Hamilton's sensitive face.

"There is something you will have to learn," he said earnestly, "something you will learn sooner or later. The problems of those who come here, whether they are from the South or from across the seas, their problems are ours. They are more than the problems of race. They are the problems of all mankind.

"Some of us live in fine houses," he went on. "We drive beautiful cars. We go to school, and we think we learn. We think we have no problems. We delude ourselves when we say their plight is not ours. Their mistakes, their ill health, their ignorance—yes, even their violence and their crimes—are problems for all of us. We cannot, we must not think that the problems are theirs alone."

As David walked home, and for a long time afterward, he thought about all that he had heard.

For the first time he realized that where he lived was considered a slum area and that people like Buck looked down on him. He knew that someday his family would move to a better neighborhood, but he hoped he would not forget that others would be left behind. It would be like moving out of the South. He did not want to forget the people there, either. Someday he would return to help them.

SEVEN

DAVID BEGAN TO SPEND MORE AND MORE of his free time at the Carver Community Center. He had gone there first with some boys from his block on a Friday evening for the Teen-Time Club.

When they arrived, a record would be put on and a few couples would be dancing. Most of the time, though, the boys just stood around and talked about sports or jazz or the girls across the room.

Some evenings there was basketball practice, and David worked hard to make the Carver team. He wasn't used to playing indoors on a hardwood floor. Still, he had speed, and by Christmas he was playing on the team as a forward with Head. Head, whose real name was John Henry Healey, was six feet two, well coordinated, and fast on his feet.

Nearly everyone who came to the Center was colored, though this was not because white people were barred. Occasionally during the afternoons, white kids who lived in the neighborhood stopped in to play Ping-Pong or work in the shop. Visiting basketball teams with all white players brought their own rooters, some of them girls. If there was a social hour after the game, they would share refreshments and listen to music, but no one would dance.

After practice one cold Monday night in January, David dressed quickly. He was hoping for a ride home with one of the other players, Billy Atkinson, who lived near him. There was no hot water in the showers, and he was eager to get home to a warm bath.

"I'll see you, fellows," Billy called over his shoulder as he headed for the door.

"Which way do you go?" David asked pointedly.

"I'm not going home direct," Billy replied, and David knew he had been rebuffed. He was sorry he had asked.

Head was tying his shoes.

"Some people I know!" he exclaimed. "Probably wheeling over to the west side. He's crazy about that girl Maybelle Reed where they had the New Year's Eve party. You know her?"

David said he did.

"Did you go to her party?" Head asked.

David shook his head. He had spent New Year's Eve at the Crutchfields with his family.

"They got a nice basement," Head went on. "She's got plenty records. Only nobody likes her much."

"Why not?" David asked, surprised.

"Her old man's a cop. When she pitches a party, he invites all his friends." Head pulled a red sweater over his head. "Millie Robinson was there," he went on, "And her old man was supposed to pick her up about one o'clock. They say when he came up and saw the squad cars he thought the house was being raided. He rushed in there, shouting. He was going to save his daughter."

David laughed with Head at the picture.

The lights were dim as David and Head left the dressing room and skirted down the side of the gym to save the varnished floor from their metal-tipped shoes.

David liked Head. He seemed like a fairly intelligent guy who desperately needed a break. Head had left school a couple of years before, and was out of a job most of the time. Once David had suggested night school to him.

"Yeah, I'm going to take that up," Head had replied, "just as soon as I get something steady to carry me along. See, if I get a job working at night, I'd have to drop out."

Sometimes, Head said, he was able to get work cooking at one of the downtown hotels. David guessed that what Head actually did was wash dishes, but he did not say so. Head always managed somehow to have enough cigarettes and spending money. The younger boys at the Center admired him for his skill as a basketball player, and he sang in a quartet, which he had organized. He was a natural leader, and had friends among the older fellows outside the Center, too.

When they walked down the steps of the building that evening and Head suggested, "Come on down the street," David willingly followed him.

"It sure is cold," he said, and pulled his scarf closer around his neck.

Under a swinging sign labeled Café, Head stopped. He pushed open the door and went in, David right behind him. In the dim light David saw two men at a marble-topped table, their empty plates before them. A fat man with his hat on the back of his head was talking loudly to the aproned proprietor behind the counter. Then he noticed a fellow, perhaps a little older than Head, sitting by himself with a cup of coffee.

"You know Hap, don't you?" Head asked.

David had never seen Hap before, but he had heard about him. He knew that Hap had been "away" and that at one time he had been the leader of a gang. A fuzzy white sports cap was pulled low over Hap's face, and he wore dark glasses. David could not see his eyes, but he could feel them looking him over.

"What you say!" Hap greeted them. "Want anything to eat?" When Head hesitated, he added, "I'm straight, man."

Head ordered a hamburger and a Coke. David did, too, but resolved to pay for his own. While they ate, Head and his friend spoke in brief exchanges that did not include David.

After they left the café, Hap led them around the corner to a car, and jumped into the driver's seat. Head opened the right-hand door and motioned for David to take the place in the middle. Hap bent and reached under the dash before he pushed the starter button and the motor pulsed into action. He backed the car away from the curb and then turned left, away from the business district.

Flipping on the radio, Head found a station with some good modern jazz. He snapped his fingers and moved his head to the steady beat. No one spoke for a while. Then Head got out his cigarettes and offered the pack to Hap and David. Hap reached toward the dashboard and, after tugging at two knobs, located the cigarette lighter which he pushed in. Suddenly David knew he was riding in a stolen car.

The three of them smoked in silence. Head was moving his hands with the rhythm of the music.

"Lots of power," he said, inhaling deeply.

"You ought to feel it," Hap replied. By now they were in the suburbs. He let the car slow until the speedometer read twenty-five. Then he pushed his foot down hard on the gas pedal, and the big machine leaped forward. It seemed to David that pressure was coming through the back of the seat. The dial registered forty—and then fifty, sixty, sixty-five. The indicator crept up to seventy, where it held steady.

Head's body stiffened. He leaned far back, his eyes closed in ecstasy. "Drive me 'til I sweat!" he cried.

David sat tense and fearful, his eyes on the road. He had to admit that Hap was a good driver. The car stayed on the right; the lights were dimmed for oncoming cars; they easily overtook and passed a truck.

Bright lights ahead illumined a highway intersection with a cluster of service stations, a diner, and a few houses. A traffic light controlled the intersection, and Hap slowed for it. The light turned from green to orange and then to red. The car braked to a stop. The music from the radio was loud.

In the instant before the light again turned green, a siren sounded close behind them. The glow of a blinking red light was reflected in the windshield. Hap drove slowly across the intersection and pulled off on the right of the pavement.

For a short space of time, David was able to tell himself that everything was all right. It really was Hap's own car, or maybe one of his friend's. It was going to be all right. Hap wasn't even trying to get away.

"Speeding!" he said, "they got us for speeding. We were going too fast."

"Shut up!" Head spoke harshly. "You don't know nothing. You don't say nothing. Not nothing."

It wasn't exciting. It wasn't even a chase. It was just bad. It was the worst thing that had ever happened to David. The police officers in the car asked only a few questions. Hap did most of the talking. A friend had loaned him the car. He didn't know the name of the friend or his address or anything like that.

Then Hap and Head and David were all three handcuffed. Hap's hands were handcuffed behind his back; David's right wrist was linked to Head's left. They were put in the patrol car, and with a short salute of the siren, the car made a U-turn through the intersection and moved swiftly back toward the city.

EIGHT

A T POLICE HEADQUARTERS, it was soon determined
that David Andrew Williams and John Henry Healey
were under eighteen and that Hap, whose real name was
Percy Johnson, was twenty-one. A different procedure
was required for booking minors, so the handcuffs were
taken off Head and David and they were led upstairs to
another office. There juvenile officers questioned them.

They sat side by side on a hard bench without a back.
A round-faced sergeant with light hair asked the questions
while a younger man, who was swarthy and lean, wrote
down the answers.

David could hardly speak. He had to struggle for
every answer, even those of the simplest sort.

"Have you ever been arrested before?" the sergeant
asked brusquely.

David hesitated.

"You might as well tell us," the sergeant said. "We'll find out anyway."

"Not really, sir." David could hardly hear his own voice.

"What do you mean 'not really'? Were you or weren't you?" the sergeant pressed him. "Were you ever picked up on anything? Were you ever booked? You don't have to have been convicted."

David did not answer. Engulfed by shame and despair, he dropped his head in his hands and closed his eyes. The officers seemed far away. Their voices seemed unreal. He was not sure what their words meant. When they asked him where he got in the car and how long he had been with Hap, he did not answer, and when they pressed him, he could only shake his head slowly and mutter, "I don't know."

With Head, it was different. The officers knew Head. They addressed him by his nickname, almost as though he were a friend. David was glad when they left him and turned their attention to Head.

Finally, the officers moved away to a counter on the opposite side of the room. David was still slumped against the wall, his eyes closed, Head close beside him, when he felt Head's elbow nudging him.

"You did good, man," Head said, congratulating him in an undertone. "They'll charge us with grand theft auto, all three of us, but we can beat it."

Grand theft auto! Beat it! We can beat it! The words filled David with terror.

Head poked him again. "You going to stick by Hap, ain't you? You ain't going chicken out?" he asked.

David did not answer.

"You been busted before?"

"Busted," David knew, meant arrested. Why did they keep asking him that? Would they call what had happened to him and his family busted? Anyway, that was down South. It shouldn't have happened. It didn't count.

"Well, have you?" Head asked again.

David shook his head.

"So they can't do nothing to you. They can't do nothing. This is the first time, and you're a juvenile. They can't do nothing more than put you on probation. That's the law in this state."

David felt some slight relief. He hoped it was true.

"Hap's got a prior. Course you probably knew that, and I'm glad you ain't going chicken out on Hap, 'cause they'd just love to put him away for a long time. And they will, too, if we don't stick together."

Head put his hand on David's shoulder. "All you got to do," he advised, "is keep on playing dumb. They can't use what you don't say against you. Besides, like I said, they can't do nothing to you. That's the law."

Head spoke rapidly in a low voice. He seemed to know all about the laws for juvenile offenders, and he was very sure of himself, referring to names of friends and cases he had heard about. He talked about judges and probation officers, and he gave detailed instructions about what to say and what not to say to inquiring "juvies," as he called the special officers on the youth detail.

"It'll be like this," he explained. "The juvies will make a case and write up a petition. Then they'll take you to court, and the judge will ask you if it's true what they say in the petition. Best thing you can do is just what you done here—play dumb. 'Cause even if you say you not guilty, they say you is. So play real dumb and say you don't know nothing, you don't remember, or something like that. Then there's the probation officer. Some of them cats try to be real cute—make you think they're on your side and they want to help you and all that jive." He took out a cigarette and matches as he talked.

"Don't let them snow you, man. They're just educated cops. They don't mean you no good unless you want to play it their way." He paused and struck a match.

"No smoking here!" the sergeant called out.

Head continued to light the cigarette as though he had not heard. He took a deep drag. Then he pushed the cigarette into David's hand.

"What you say, sir?" he asked innocently as he looked up.

The sergeant moved quickly from behind the counter, and David cringed, expecting a blow. Frightened, he dropped the cigarette on the floor and covered his face with his hands.

But no blow came.

"Pick it up!" the officer ordered. As David bent over, he heard, "Not you! I mean Head!"

"I don't put nothing on the floor, Sarge," Head said calmly, his arms folded. "I don't pick nothing up."

"I did it," David said hurriedly. "I didn't mean to. I'll get it."

"No!" The officer's leg blocked David, and his hand grabbed the back of Head's neck. The muscles of Head's face tightened with pain as his body was forced slowly forward. David watched the officer's white fingers pressing hard against Head's dark skin. He drew away, hating the cop. He hated the other cop who was standing there watching, waiting for Head to move. He hated them all. White folks!

"Pick it up!" The sergeant's words came through clenched teeth. David was glad when Head's right hand reached out and retrieved the still-smoking cigarette butt.

"On your feet now," the sergeant commanded. Head was half turned, half pushed toward the hall. The second officer flicked a switch on the intercom and reported, "One coming in for lockup."

David was sure that now Head would be beaten. He had never witnessed such defiance of law. He had never before seen a Negro refuse to carry out a white man's order. He listened fearfully, expecting to hear blows and cries of pain. It wasn't worth it, he decided. Head shouldn't have asked for it like that. This was one of the times when Head should have done what he was told, knowing what a white man would do when he had the chance.

The sergeant came back, half-smiling. "He can smoke back there," he said to David.

At that moment there was the sound of more footsteps in the passage. David turned to see his father coming through the door with a policeman in blue overcoat and cap.

David saw in his father's face an anguish that had nothing to do with physical pain or beating or threat of death.

"Son!" Mr. Williams exclaimed.

"They'll tell you about it," the policeman said. Taking Mr. Williams by the arm, he turned him toward the counter.

"Yes sir," the swarthy officer said, rising to his feet. "Are you this boy's father?"

David heard the questions the officers asked his father, and he heard the answers his father gave, and then he heard his father's questions and officers' account of the arrest, the fact that the car was stolen, and their very low opinion of both of David's companions.

"If your boy's the kind of kid you say he is," the sergeant said, "if he's a decent kid, then he sure is running with the wrong kind. Sometimes they do, you know. It wouldn't be so bad if the good guys didn't try to act like the bad guys. You know what I mean?"

"You know, Mr. Williams," the other officer said, "this boy of yours hasn't been very cooperative. Not at first, anyway. He clammed up. Looked like he was trying to cover up for his pals. He should know what these hoodlums are like, both of them."

"You mean he wouldn't talk?" Mr. Williams asked in disbelief. "He wouldn't answer questions?" He turned to look at his son, but David did not return his gaze.

"Aw, it doesn't matter," the sergeant shrugged. "But under 'attitude,' we're going to have to spell it out— 'sullen, withheld information, uncooperative.' Know what I mean?"

"I guess I do, but I'm surprised." Mr. Williams shook his head. "I just don't understand it. I can't understand it."

"You and the other fathers!" The sergeant laughed. "Nobody understands nowadays what makes juvenile delinquents, but I bet your father did—and I bet he knew how to handle his son, too."

Mr. Williams did not join in the laughter. "May I talk to my boy?" he asked.

"Sure, all you want," the sergeant replied. "You can take him home with you. Only have him in court, let's see"—he checked a calendar. "Probably the eighteenth. Have him in juvenile court when they call for him. That's the second floor of the county building. You'll get a notice."

Mr. Williams gave his solemn assurance that he would be there with David. He was then told to sign the "Promise to Appear" form, and he reached eagerly for the pen, but his hand shook so that he was ashamed of his poor writing. They would think he was an illiterate, he thought.

He crossed the room to David and stood before him; David did not look up. Mr. Williams laid his hand on his son's shoulder. "We're going home, son," he said.

David half raised his face. His father spoke again, "We'll talk about it later. They say we can go now."

David motioned with his head toward the hall. "They're doing something bad to my friend," he said.

Mr. Williams quickly sat down on the bench beside him. "What? What are you saying?"

"They took Head, John Henry. They beat him up. They'll try to kill him. You got to do something, Pa. You know what they do."

Mr. Williams rose. His voice was hard as he spoke to the sergeant, "What about the others?"

"Oh, we had to put that Healey boy in the back." The sergeant was casual about it; too casual, it seemed. "His folks won't be coming down for him. There's only his mother, and she can't do anything with him."

"They hurt him," David blurted out.

"Well, we had to use a little restraint. He broke bad." The sergeant got to his feet. "Want to speak to him? Come on, both of you."

David and his father followed the officer out the door and down the hall. They turned right into another corridor and finally stopped before a gate of heavy steel bars. Here the officer summoned a guard. "They want to see Healey," he explained.

David figured it was a trick, and he wanted to turn back. Maybe they would all be held, he thought wildly. The guard slid a thick metal key into the lock and then swung the gate open. David and his father walked through, and the bars clanged behind them. Now David could see dimly lighted barred sections, stretching on both sides of the corridor. The bunks in most of them were unoccupied, though some held blanketed forms of men who might have been asleep.

Before the last section on the left, the guard called, "Healey, on your feet!"

David saw that, inside, only one bunk was occupied. On it a figure stirred, and Head turned his face toward his friend. He swung his bare feet to the floor, stretched, and walked forward, smiling.

"What you say, man? This your daddy? You going home?" Head asked.

This time it was surprise that kept David from speaking. He could only nod.

"Don't forget what I told you. You know." Head

looked at Mr. Williams and back to David. "You doing all right, man. Say, you got any smokes? Let me hold them. You can get plenty more."

As Head reached out his hand, David removed a pack of cigarettes from his pocket. The guard nodded and took the pack from David, then passed it to his prisoner.

David did not look at his father as he turned and walked away.

David Williams had never lied to his father. He would have admitted that when he was a little kid he had sometimes twisted answers and evaded questions, not telling all the truth about just where he had been or some such, but he had never really lied. He might not have been able to explain the reasons for this. The main reason was that it had not been necessary. His father was not what you would call a hard man, unlike the fathers of some of David's friends. He was intuitive and understanding, and he seemed always, or almost always, very reasonable. Perhaps the time would come when David would deliberately tell his father a lie. Perhaps this might be the time.

On the way home that night, riding in the faithful old family Chevrolet, David explained what had happened; then he answered, as well as he could, his father's questions.

Yes, he had known Head for a while, and he had thought he was all right; that is, he had never heard anything bad about him. Yes, he knew that you couldn't always tell who might be a juvenile delinquent or even a criminal. No, he just hadn't known Hap well enough to know he didn't have a car. Even some of the boys still going to school had their own cars—ones they had bought themselves or old cars of their parents. Yes, of course, if he had known the car was stolen, he would never have gone in it with the others. All of this, which was true, he told his father. He did not tell him that he had seen Hap reach under the dash before he pushed the starter button, nor did he speak of Hap's difficulty in locating the cigarette lighter. In fact, David said nothing to indicate that he was anything but a completely innocent bystander. He knew he was not telling the whole truth.

As they stopped for the last traffic light before reaching home, Mr. Williams said, "Your mother is going to be very upset."

"Couldn't we not tell her?" David asked. "Or maybe not tell her everything?"

"Not hardly." The light turned green, and the car rolled forward. "Not hardly. The policemen came to the house and she heard it from them. I don't see how we could keep anything from her," he concluded with sorrow. He put on the brake and drew up to the curb in front of the house. "It will hurt her, but one good thing, it won't be like you were really guilty. She'll understand that."

"Pa, let's go on. Don't stop. I'd like to talk."

"We can talk in the house."

"No, I'd rather talk to you first. Can't we just drive a little?"

Mr. Williams looked questioningly at David, then started the motor. He could see that his son was miserably unhappy, and he sensed that there was more to tell. They rode several blocks in silence.

Finally he spoke. "What is it, son? Why don't you tell me?"

"It's no use," David muttered. "I might as well admit it. They're going to say I'm guilty anyway."

Mr Williams pulled up so abruptly by the side of the road that the tires squealed.

"What did you say?"

"I don't mean I'm guilty, but I can't prove I'm not," David said.

"You can prove you never stole anything before, and this fellow that stole the car has a record. Besides, you were at the game tonight until almost the time the three of you were picked up. You sure don't have to admit to something you didn't do."

"It's no use, Pa. John Henry was telling me. They'll charge all three of us anyway, and we might as well admit it and get it over with. They'll put me on probation, that's all."

"So that's what your friend told you," Mr. Williams said. "That you'd all three go down together? These toughs! These hoodlums! I guess they'd like to have you tied up with them. Don't do it, son! Don't do it!"

In his desperation Mr. Williams held tightly to David's arm, trying to arouse him into a realization of what a plea of guilty implied. David did not argue, but he did not agree with his father. He felt defeated and hopeless.

Mr. Williams, his voice taut, spoke of the necessity for David to tell the truth, of the evils of having a record as a thief. He forced David to recognize that Head's plan was for the sake of Hap who might otherwise be sent to prison. David knew that his father was right. It would be bad to have a record. He listened to all that his father said, glad that he was not scolding, only advising and urging, though he was clearly trying to get David to do what Head would call "finking out."

"I'll get a lawyer," Mr. Williams said. "He'll fight for you. He'll probably want to get your case tried separately. He'll speak for you. He'll show the judge that you're not a juvenile delinquent. He'll prove it. Everybody will know that you don't have anything in common with the others."

Out of his bitterness, David spoke. "Pa, that's what we'd like to think," he said. "Maybe you don't know, but I'm learning. It's just the same, Pa. It's just the same as down South. I've got plenty in common with those others. We're all colored together, and the whites will prove we're guilty together."

"Don't say that!" The back of Mr. Williams's hand smashed across David's mouth. "Shut up, I won't hear it! Don't tell me that what we went through in South Town has got to happen all over again. It ain't so. There's law here. I got a decent job. You're going to a decent school. You've got a chance to be somebody here. To live decent. Don't tell me it's just the same!"

The blow hurt. David's lip was cut, but the hurt was more than just that. David had not been hit by his father since he was a young boy, and never before had his father struck him with such anger.

But David was sure of his point. His father was blind, just dumb fool blind. He would prove it.

"Pa, listen to me! Will you listen? Look at where we're

living. Can you get a decent apartment anywhere in North Town? They got lots of places advertised, but not for us. Even to buy. Can you buy any but the old rundown houses, or pay double if you get something halfway decent? You know you've been saying that yourself."

"But we're still better off. And we will get something," Mr. Williams insisted.

"But you don't know how it is—How they act like they're your friend, and then as soon as they get the chance they're ready to give you a dirty deal. I've seen it at school, on the football field, and every place, and I know that judge'll just take one look and say, 'These guys are guilty.' It's no use, I tell you." David was almost crying. But his father was determined to change his son's thinking.

"Boy," he said, "if I thought you were right, I'd pack up and go to the farthest county in Mississippi, and I'd hire out as a field hand for the rest of my life. It ain't so, I tell you. And you got to learn better. I'll prove it. You'll see I'm right. Tomorrow morning, first thing, I'm going to call a lawyer. That real-estate man, Mr. Taylor, is a lawyer and a good one, they say. I'll phone him from the job. We're going to fight this thing!"

He reached over and started the car. A few moments later he pulled up at the curb in front of the drab two-story house in which they lived. After turning off the ignition, he sat gazing straight ahead with both hands on the wheel.

"Dave," he said, "I'm sorry I hit you. I truly am. I never meant to strike a child of mine in anger, and you're not even a child. You're most a man now. You got a right to your opinion, I guess, but if I thought you were right I'd be the most disappointed black man that ever lived."

As they walked up the steps, Mr. Williams held his son's arm. They opened the door to the dimly lit hall, and from the apartment above came the wail of a blues song.

Before Mr. Williams put the key in his own lock, he turned again to David.

"You don't have to tell your ma what I done—in the car. Maybe later, sometime, I'll tell her."

"Don't tell her, Pa," David begged. "I hope you don't ever tell her."

NINE

Buck Taylor first heard about David's arrest the following evening at the dinner table. Although Mr. Taylor was an ethical lawyer and never discussed the confidential business of his clients even with his wife, the affair of the Williams boy was now public knowledge.

Mr. Taylor's law practice was not large since his real-estate business gave him ample income, and demanded most of his time. However, he took pride in his knowledge of the law and in his personal contacts with North Town judges and politicians. He sometimes felt that his son did not show him proper respect, that in his own house he was a prophet without honor. So, when he talked at home about a case, he consciously tried to emphasize the fact that in the halls of justice he was a man of status and that white people, as well as colored, looked upon him with respect.

"The police picked up three fellows in a stolen car last night," he volunteered at an appropriate break in the conversation. "One was an old customer and two were juveniles. The father of one of the boys has asked me to represent him."

He put salt and pepper on his meat. "The boy came to see me this afternoon. Bruce, maybe you know him." Mr. Taylor wanted to learn what kind of reputation David had at school, so he added, "Says he goes to Central. Name is Williams, David Williams."

"Yes," Buck acknowledged, "I know him. He's new— from the South."

"I have to go to juvenile court with him on Thursday. What's he like? Get into any trouble in school?"

Buck told what he knew, believing his report to be completely honest. He mentioned the trouble on the football field, adding that David ran around with fellows from the east side. He was kind of dumb, he said, and real Southern.

"But they say," he added, "he gets pretty good grades. Of course, he doesn't go out for athletics and student activities."

"Usually I don't like these juvenile cases," Mr. Taylor said. "They have special laws of procedure. The judge runs his court informally and doesn't follow the rules of evidence."

Mr. Taylor related some of his experiences in juvenile court; then he went back to David. "Now the way this boy talks! It's as though he were afraid of something," he said.

"Maybe he belongs to a gang," Buck guessed. "Those gangs are pretty tight."

"I asked about that." His father shook his head. "He says he doesn't, and yet he keeps avoiding the issues. Says he doesn't remember. I think he's trying to protect the others."

"Who are the others? Maybe I know them."

"There's a John Henry Healey and a Percy Johnson."

Buck smiled at the names. "Yes," he said, "I know Head—that's what they call Healey. And everybody knows Percy Johnson, but they call him Hap. Anybody might get hurt calling him Percy. He hates it. Lots of the boys are afraid of him. With Hap in it, I can see what Williams might be afraid of. Maybe he's got good reason."

"What are his people like? The new boy's, I mean," asked Mrs. Taylor, who was serving dessert. "Do you know anything at all about his family?"

"Oh, they're just some more common Southern people, I guess, living over on the east side like the rest of them," Buck answered.

"Bruce, I don't know what you mean by that." Mr. Taylor was annoyed. "Maybe you think 'some more common Southern people' are not worth bothering with. When I was your age, I lived in the South—yes, and on a Georgia farm."

"But, Daddy, you say yourself that these newcomers are ignorant and don't know how to live. You're always having to help them. Getting them out of jail, like now, and finding them homes they can buy and arranging their mortgages."

"But that's my work," Mr. Taylor said. "And I get paid for getting them out of jail, and I make a commission every time I sell a house or place a mortgage."

"I bet they thought they were coming to the Promised Land when they left down there," Buck said, laughing.

"I don't understand you, Bruce." Mr. Taylor looked at his son with surprise. "Maybe you're too integrated already. You know, the Jews have an expression, some of them, that is. They say of another Jew who has succeeded and who now looks with scorn on the struggling poorer Jews, 'He forgets the ghetto.' I'm afraid many of us with some success and some schooling 'forget the ghetto.' "

Buck did not want to be offensive, but his father had always invited discussion, and now when Buck could not agree he felt he should say so.

"I, for one, would be very happy to forget the ghetto, and the old tales of slavery days and the South and Jim Crow and discrimination. I'm doing all right. At school everybody treats me O.K. I'd just as soon forget that I'm a Negro."

"Oh, Bruce!" Mrs. Taylor's hand went to her throat. "How can you talk like that?"

Mr. Taylor laid down his fork, marshaling his arguments. Buck turned to his mother. It was easier to talk to her than to his father.

"I mean it," he stated vehemently. "Around here we're always talking about race and Negroes, race pride and Negro history. So what? Why can't we just be Americans? This is a democracy. I'm a senior at Central High School. My father's a lawyer. I'm just like hundreds of others at school. I don't see why I should make something different out of myself."

Mr. Taylor shook his head sadly. "Bruce, if I've led you to believe that by going to Central you can overcome bigotry and race prejudice, then I'm sorry. And if you believe your daddy is the big businessman and the eminent lawyer that means success in American life, then, boy, you're so wrong. Your daddy is a very little fellow who scarcely makes enough to live decently and to plan for the future of his family. And let's face it." Mr. Taylor raised his hand in protest as Bruce tried to interrupt. "I make my living off the people you would like to forget. The parents of your white friends at Central don't come to me for help. They aren't even aware of me. And you're going to find out that white people won't let you forget your color, no matter how much you want to. And you'll have no ghetto to remember. Some people get lost like that."

The conversation was interrupted by a telephone call for Mr. Taylor, and Buck took the opportunity to excuse himself. He wanted to see Jeanette and be the first to tell her the news about David. He bounded upstairs and slipped into his new award sweater with the scarlet C and two scarlet stripes on the left sleeve. He knew it looked well on him.

"Don't forget your coat," his mother called. "It's cold out tonight." But Buck insisted he'd be warm enough in his sweater. He ran all the way to Jeanette's house.

Mr. Lenoir opened the door at his ring, and led the way back to the dining room where the family was finishing dinner.

"Hello, Buck," Mrs. Lenoir said smiling. "Pull up a chair and have some dessert with us."

Mrs. Lenoir was very dark in color. She had strong, sharp features that softened when she smiled. Her hair was pulled back from her face and fastened neatly in a French twist. Jeanette looked very much like her.

Mr. Lenoir, who sat at the head of the table, was much lighter than his wife. He might have been a Creole. Jeanette's older sister was light, too, and could easily have passed as white.

The Lenoirs liked Buck. Mr. Lenoir admired Buck's father and gave him generous praise. All of them thought it was wonderful that Buck did so well at school. Both Mr. and Mrs. Lenoir welcomed him to their home and considered him good company for their younger daughter.

Although Buck announced that he had just finished dinner at his house, Mrs. Lenoir went to the kitchen and returned with a dish of peach cobbler topped with ice cream. He accepted with only a minimum of protest.

In reply to their questions Buck answered that his family was well, that school was all right, and that he was not going out for basketball.

"I got behind during the football season," he explained. "Can't afford to have any low grades this year."

"Have you decided about going into the law?" Mr. Lenoir asked.

"Not altogether," Buck replied. "Lawyers have to do a lot of work they don't get paid for—like for those people over in the slums, getting them out of trouble, jail, and all that."

"He means, Daddy"—Jeanette smiled, but she was serious—"he means like the people who live on the east side, maybe along Sixth Street in those flats."

"Yes, that's what I mean." Buck spoke easily, sure of himself. "My dad's just been hired to defend one of them—a fellow lives over there, goes to our school. Jeanette knows him, David Williams. Grand theft he was arrested for, with two other tough guys."

Jeanette stiffened. "Not David!" she said. "Not David Williams!"

"Yeah, David Williams. Some kind of friend you want to be responsible for."

"Why, we know David," Mrs. Lenoir said. "His parents seem to be very nice people."

"I guess I'd better go see Williams," Mr. Lenoir said. "Maybe there's something I can do."

The Lenoir family's reaction was not at all what Buck had expected. They pressed him for details. Mr. Lenoir said he must call the Williams home, and Jeanette gave him the number. They went into the hall to listen while he spoke to Mr. Williams. "Suppose I come over. I'd like to talk with you about it," Buck heard him say.

His wife helped him into his overcoat. "Please tell Mrs. Williams to phone if there is anything I can do," she said.

There was a sudden silence after the front door slammed; then they heard the hum of the car motor. Mrs. Lenoir went to the kitchen to start the dishes, leaving Jeanette and Buck to look questioningly at each other.

"Wouldn't a juvenile delinquency record spoil David's chances for college?" Jeanette asked.

"College! He's not going to college. He'll never see the inside of a college."

"Buck, you talk about David Williams as if you really knew something bad about him. As a matter of fact, I don't believe you've ever taken the time to talk to him. You don't know a thing about him."

"You know, don't you! You've spent plenty of time

with him, I bet. Even your folks. I guess you've had him and his family right here in your own home. I can't understand it."

"You don't want to understand it, Buck."

"There's nothing I want to understand about a guy who is as dumb as he is and who goes on the field attacking players just because they're white and who runs with a pack of hoodlums and gets arrested for car theft. He's not my kind and I think too much of myself to get down to his level."

"You wouldn't even ask him about what happened on the field that day. Well, I did. I asked Al Kirinski, too, and some of the others. The only thing David failed to do was speak up for himself. And about his family. My folks invited them over during the holidays. His mother is a very sweet person who used to teach school in the South. She and my mother have a lot in common. They're the same kind of people. They had trouble in the South. My father had trouble, too, and that was why we left down there."

"Then why don't they get out of the slums? Why do they stay there?"

"It takes money to buy a house. You should know that. They don't have enough money for a down payment on the kind of house they want. They're trying to make out. They're doing the best they can for now, and they know that people like you—yes, people like us on the west side—look down on them. Well, there isn't much difference. My father says we're all newcomers, only some are newer than others. And he says all of America is made up of newcomers. Somebody wrote a book showing that the United States is just one mass of minorities, only the Negroes are especially marked because of their color."

"I've heard all that before. All about the race problem, and I'm sick of it."

"Yes, I know you are. But there's David Williams. And he's our problem now."

"Not mine. You can have him and his problems!"

"You're selfish, Buck. You really don't care what happens to David, do you?"

"Why should I? What are you all getting so worked up about? Your dad going running over there to the east side? My dad talking about remembering the ghetto?"

Jeanette's sister, passing through the hall on her way upstairs, laughingly suggested they go sit in the living room and finish their argument. Jeanette claimed they weren't arguing, but Buck knew that they were.

He followed her into the living room and, still standing, turned and asked, "You like David Williams, don't you?"

Jeanette's eyebrows rose even higher than usual. "I hadn't thought about it." She paused. "About liking him, that is, but I guess I do think he's a very nice person." She looked defiantly at Buck. "Yes, I like David, and I like his folks."

When Buck left Jeanette's house it was after nine o'clock. The winter wind was sharp, but even though he was coatless, he walked home with slow steps, his mind deep in thought.

TEN

THE THURSDAY MORNING THAT DAVID was to appear in court started almost like a Sunday in the Williams home. It was like a Sunday, but it was also very different. The evening before, David's mother had ironed a clean white shirt for him and checked to see if his best suit needed pressing. She had also decided that he needed a haircut and sent him to the barbershop.

On Thursday morning, they all got up very early and, after breakfast, David and his parents dressed in their Sunday clothes. Mr. Williams was taking the day off from his job. Betty Jane had to go to school like any other day, and she complained loudly. Otherwise, they had little to say. Mr. Taylor had told them to be in court by nine thirty, but Mr. Williams planned to be there before nine.

Throughout the long night David had slept fitfully. He

tossed from side to side, his mind refusing to let him rest.

He knew his father wanted him not only to deny he had stolen the car but also to say that he was different from Head and Hap, that really they were not his friends—in short, that he was a "good" boy. David felt that such talk would be disloyal. They were three colored boys in trouble together, and he must not betray them.

The court would be like the situation on the school football field. The white judge would inevitably say, "You might as well go, too!" But David was determined he would not say that he did not know the car was stolen. He would not "chicken out."

He had been puzzled by Mr. Cooper, the probation officer, when he came to visit him at home. Mr. Cooper was colored, and if Head had not warned him David would have thought he was a good guy.

He had asked David all sorts of questions about himself and his family, and David had answered freely until he was queried about the night he was arrested. But then when he refused to talk, the probation officer surprised him.

"Look, David," he said. "You don't have to talk about it. You don't have to tell me a thing. I'm not trying to get a confession out of you."

His parents thought the probation officer was a fine young man who really wanted to help. David could not be sure.

He wasn't sure about Mr. Taylor, either.

Mr. Taylor wasn't like any of the lawyers David had seen in the movies or on television or read about in books.

He was just like someone you knew. He talked just as David's own father talked about the other fellows. They were no good, he said. They were bad company. Well, David told himself, bad company is no excuse. Sure, he had suspected, even before that night, that Head had some kind of a record. So he was bad company. So Billy Atkinson was good company, and Atkinson was on the team, but he had said that night he was going the other way, while Head had at least been friendly enough to extend an invitation. . . . If it had been Head driving his father's car that night, he would have called all the players together and taken them home.

David had left South Town with such high hopes. He had believed that someday he'd have a medical degree and that he'd return to the hills of Pocohantas County and set up his office in a house like the one his father had owned there beside Route One. Only it would be a bigger house with waiting rooms and an operating room and one or two other rooms, like a small hospital, where some of his patients could remain for treatment and care.

Maybe now it would never happen.

He was sick, almost physically sick as he thought of it, but he could not turn his back on Head. He could not "chicken out."

It was bad, but there was nothing else he could do.

This was the decision he reached in the dark.

With the coming of morning, however, he wasn't so sure.

By nine o'clock that morning David and his parents were seated in the waiting room on the second floor of the county building. The county employees came in noisy groups up the stairs and exchanged greetings as they opened the doors to their offices and began their work for the day. At nine fifteen Mr. Williams spoke to a clerk who told him to wait until his son's case was called.

The waiting room filled rapidly with parents and their children. Just before nine thirty a uniformed officer appeared in the doorway. Behind him a line of boys filed slowly past the door. David recognized Head who turned to search the faces in the crowded waiting room. When he saw David, he smiled and lifted a circled thumb and forefinger.

How do you do what's right? How do you really know right from wrong? Should you tell the whole truth or hold back part? Do you save yourself by letting all the blame fall on the other fellow? And if you can't help him anyway, is there any harm in helping yourself?

Right and wrong! He had always thought they were easy to tell apart, like black and white. Right and wrong, they were supposed to be opposites. But were they so different? Weren't right and wrong very close to each other? And black and white? Fellows like Alonzo Wells and Jimmy Hines seemed very sure that white people were bad and hateful, that all of them were trying somehow to league together to make it hard for colored people. Head was like that, too. But Head thought everyone was against him because nobody, white or colored, cared about him.

At last, Mr. Taylor and Mr. Cooper appeared and beckoned to the Williamses. They crossed the waiting room and stepped into the wide corridor to talk.

"We've been talking about the case," Mr. Taylor said, without wasting any time in formal greetings. "The probation officer is not willing to recommend dismissal. However, I'm prepared to argue the matter in court."

David's mother was holding his arm. He felt her hand tighten.

"It's not a matter of what I'm willing to do," Mr. Cooper explained. "It is what the situation calls for. We're trying to think of what is best for David Williams. It looks like he needs the court's help."

Mr. Taylor spoke of the lack of evidence, of David's good grades in school, and of the damaging effects of a court record. The probation officer spoke of the need for guidance and of the difficulties in adjusting to urban living. David felt as though they were discussing someone who wasn't there.

"After all, you know," the probation officer concluded, "I only offer my recommendation. The court, the judge himself, will make the decision."

They waited for more than an hour before their turn came. As they entered the courtroom, David looked about him with awe. The walls were paneled in dark walnut, and the judges' bench, a high platform of polished wood, loomed imposingly at the front of the chamber. Above the platform, on the wall, hung an American flag; beneath it and separated from the rest of the room by a railing, there was a long table.

A uniformed guard led David down the aisle and stationed him inside the railing. Mr. Taylor stood at his side, and his parents stood behind him. Seated at the table facing them was a gray-haired man. He was talking earnestly to Mr. Cooper. At the other end of the table sat the sergeant David had seen in the police station, another man in uniform, and two women. The seats in the main part of the room were all empty.

A side door opened, and a guard brought in Head. He directed him to stand next to David.

"Does this boy have any people here?" the gray-haired man asked.

"Your Honor, I called the case in the waiting room, but no one answered," the attendant replied.

"His mother was cited, your Honor," Mr. Cooper said. "I served her myself."

"Perhaps she's been delayed," the judge said, looking about him. "Let's see now. Who is present? You are David Williams, I take it, and Mr. and Mrs. Williams." He paused as Mr. Taylor gave his name. "Yes, the counsel for the Williams boy. How about the Healey minor? Are you representing him?"

"No, your Honor, I was not asked to," Mr. Taylor replied. The judge turned to Head.

"You are John Henry Healey?" Head nodded. "Well, John, what about your mother? She knows where you are, I suppose. Has she been to see you?"

"Yes sir, Judge. She came to see me in detention. She said she'd be here. She's late, I guess."

"I presume she's on her way. Mr. Bolden," he addressed one of the guards, "better alert them outside for—let's see—" He glanced at his papers. "Mrs. Annie Healey. Tell them to send her right in."

The judge turned back to his audience. "I am Judge Winston G. Burnett," he said clearly, "and I believe you know Mr. Cooper, the probation officer, and perhaps you know Sergeant Delaney of the Youth Detail. The special court officer is Sergeant Swanson. Mrs. O'Brian is here, representing the school board, and Miss Oliphant is our reporter.

"I want you people to be seated now. I don't want you to be uncomfortable." He waited while they all took their places. "Not that this isn't serious business. It is very serious, and it is important that we act with wisdom. I am not sure what your previous experience has been, or what you may have been told before you came here. There are some basic concepts which I want to make clear. What we do and say later will be within the framework of these concepts.

"First, I want to say that, although we hold our hearings privately and without formality, this is primarily a court of law within the American concept of justice, and there are certain rights which have been handed down through generations. All of those rights are observed here. No one has to give evidence against himself, and every person has the full right to face and question those who bring evidence against him. Any person brought into this court has the right to have counsel, a lawyer to speak and to act in his behalf."

The judge paused and looked at the faces before him as though he wondered whether they understood him. "Yet there are differences between this court and our criminal courts," he went on. "In this court no one is being prosecuted. We do not have a defendant here, because these boys are not charged with any crime. We have no prosecuting attorney. The simple fact is that we have a petition asking this court to assume responsibility for the future of these minors, because allegedly there is grave danger that they will lead lives of crime.

"Since the arrest of the minors and their companion the probation officer has made an investigation and he has submitted a report to the court. . . ."

The judge paused as the door opened and a guard announced Mrs. Healey. She was a tall, plain woman, shabbily dressed.

"Come in, Mrs. Healey," the judge said. "We are just getting started." The attendant led her down to the front row and motioned her toward a seat. She glanced toward the judge, but her attention was on John Henry, who did not look up. She took a seat one removed from his.

"I'm sorry, Judge," she said. "Look like I just couldn't make it so early."

"Well, we're glad you are here. I was just explaining about this court."

"Oh yessir, Judge. I heard all that before. You know me and John Henry, we been here before. I heard all that already."

"Very well then. Mr. Swanson, will you read the petitions?"

The officer stood up to read the formal documents, and David gave them his full attention. He had been surprised to hear the judge say what he did. Now he was even more surprised to hear nothing about grand theft or about any charges really, although the petition said that he and Head had been riding in a stolen car. Earlier the probation officer, too, had said that he was not being charged with a crime, but David had simply not believed him. The two petitions were just alike except for the fact that John Henry Healey was already a ward of the Juvenile Court. The officer sat down, and Judge Burnett thanked him.

"Do you understand the petitions?" the judge then asked the boys.

Mr. Taylor got to his feet.

"Your Honor, if it please the court," he said, "I should like to offer a motion."

"Counsel," the judge replied, "if this is to be the usual motion for dismissal, I will suggest that you withhold it. I don't think such a motion would be appropriate at this time. It would be denied."

The lawyer took his seat, but it was clear that he was not pleased.

"John, you have been here before. Do you understand why you are here now?" the judge asked him.

"I understand all right. It's grand theft auto. Only I didn't do it."

"Young man, did you listen while the petition was being read?" Head nodded. "And don't you know that nothing was said about grand theft auto?"

"Yessir. I heard what it said all right. But that's what it means. You know I been here before."

"I suppose you do think you know." The judge frowned and looked down at his papers. When he glanced up again, he said, "You've been on probation nearly a year. Do you think it has done you any good?"

"Yessir. I been doing all right."

"Now in this case, did you know you were in a car which had been stolen?"

"Oh, no, sir. That's what I was saying. I didn't know anything about it. When they picked me up, this boy told me it was his old man's car."

David thought he must not have heard right.

The judge's face showed no change, but Mr. Cooper's face showed new interest. Behind him, David heard his father stir.

"Would you want to tell us how it happened?" the judge asked.

Head leaned forward in his chair. His words came easily.

"Well, it was like this, see. I was playing basketball, and when I was going home, walking down Sixth Street, I see this boy, David. I already know him from playing basketball with him, and he blows the horn at me and said, Do I want a ride home? And I figured it was cold, but before I get in the car I ask him, and he say it's his daddy's car. So I get in, see, and then he say, Why don't we go out for a ride? And then he asked Hap, that's Percy Johnson, see, Do he want to drive? And Hap say he'll try her, and that's when the patrol come up behind us, and Hap didn't even try to get away 'cause he figured like me that it was his daddy's car, see, so he wasn't worried."

Mr. Taylor had been standing throughout Head's speech. When Head paused, he interrupted, "Your Honor, I object. This witness is making charges; he is giving testimony which is not true. He may in fact be committing perjury, and I respectfully move that the testimony of this witness be stricken from the record."

"Counsel," Judge Burnett replied, "I recognize that after participating in usual court procedure you find this unusual, but I repeat, there are no charges in this court, and the court is privileged to hear whatever the parties wish to say. This minor has not been sworn, so what he says cannot be held as perjury. Objection overruled."

Leaning back in his chair, the judge thoughtfully fixed his gaze upon each member of the group.

"And again I call to your attention the fact that this court exists not to prosecute but to help young people who are in trouble, and it is important that we hear what they have to say, true or false."

Mr. Taylor sat down with a frown.

"Now, back to John," the judge continued, "or do you like to be called John Henry?"

"They mostly call me Head."

It seemed to David that Head was enjoying himself. Under questioning, he explained that David had left the Center early that Monday evening and that they were not really close friends so he did not know what kind of car David's family owned.

The judge turned next to David, but he did not ask him about the stolen car. Instead he asked how David was getting along in school and whether he still wanted to become a physician. Then he turned to David's father and asked him about his job at the Foundation Iron and Machine Works and about his apartment, whether it was adequate for his family of four. After listening carefully, he said, as though it were the most important matter in the entire discussion, that he hoped Mr. Williams would soon be able to find a better place to live, a place where David could have his own room because every boy needed one.

"John," the judge addressed Head, "I don't know whether you made up your story to try to help your friend Johnson or to save yourself. I only wish I could make you understand that you have been told the truth in this courtroom. We want to help you; you don't have to lie to us. You have been on probation, and apparently you have not learned from the guidance and counseling of your probation officer. So we are going to continue you as a ward of the court, but instead of letting you remain in your mother's home, we are going to place you in a forestry camp where you will work regularly and hard, and live within a regulated order. How long you remain there will depend on your own behavior and development. You will have opportunities to develop some skills, and, if your conduct is good, you'll be granted certain privileges. This is not a correctional institution but a training unit, and we hope you will accept the training and not later have to undergo correction."

The judge cleared his throat. "David Andrew Williams," he pronounced solemnly.

David got to his feet, his knees trembling.

"We have gone thoroughly into your case," the judge said. "The court is inclined to believe that your father and your mother are able to provide you with the right kind of upbringing. The probation officer's report gives quite a full picture of you and your family."

"We do, however," the judge went on, "admonish you to follow such a course as your father must have followed. You have many advantages and many opportunities. Your parents are trying to make a good life for you. Make your companions the boys who are struggling for something good. This court is expressing the community's confidence that you can contribute something of value. We hope that confidence is not being misplaced. To the parents of the minor, the court observes that you have brought this boy a long way, through many hazards. This is one more; perhaps it is the most serious. We hope it will prove to be the last of this type.

"For the record, the allegations are found to be true; the petition is sustained; the minor is admonished; and the case is dismissed."

ELEVEN

On their way home, after the hearing, David's father said very little.

"The judge was very kind. He explained, and you could understand," his mother commented. "I felt sorry for Mrs. Healey. She said she understood, but I don't believe she did. Her son is lost. Maybe she doesn't know it, or if she does, she doesn't know what to do about it."

David was numb with relief that he had not been put on probation. He knew that both his parents felt relieved, but that they were also still unhappy over the whole episode. He was ready to admit that the hearing had been fair and without prejudice. Doubtless, Judge Burnett was an exceptional white man, he decided.

Once home, David decided to go to school. If he hurried, he could make his afternoon classes. While he changed into a pair of khaki pants and a wool shirt, his mother fixed some sandwiches. Mr. Williams shook his head at the suggestion of lunch and went into his bedroom, closing the door behind him. They knew he was having one of his headaches.

When school was over that afternoon, David waited outside the main door, hoping he would not miss Jeanette in the crowd of students that poured out of the building. When he finally caught a glimpse of her, she was with Maybelle and some other girls. Laughing and talking, she started down the wide stairs, without seeing him. A knitted red cap was pulled low over her head, framing her face above the turned-up collar of her white overcoat. She was prettier than any girl he had ever known, David decided.

One of the other girls saw David and spoke to Jeanette who raised a gloved hand in greeting. Then she excused herself and ran down the rest of the steps to meet him.

Her eyes were wide with questions, but her smile was restrained, as if she were afraid of what she might hear.

"I'm glad you waited," she said. "Tell me, how was it?"

He reassured her immediately by saying that his case had been dismissed, and then he told her everything that had happened. At the corner where she usually caught her bus, she announced she wanted to keep on walking.

"What's going to happen to Head?" she asked.

"I don't know," David said. "You know when you think about it, he really hasn't got much of a chance. No father, and his mother can't be much help. In the court-room he never looked at his mother, but when we were leaving and the guard was taking him away, he waved to me and he was smiling. I can't even be mad at him for the way he tried to put all the weight on me."

"Do you think," Jeanette asked, "that for some reason he was trying to hurt you?"

"No, it couldn't be that."

"Would his story really have helped his other friend?"

"No, but maybe he thought it would. Mr. Taylor told my father that Hap was sure to be convicted in the adult court."

They had walked almost all the way to Jeanette's house. As they crossed the bridge over the parkway, they stopped and looked down at the flow of traffic.

"I'll bet your father's glad it's over," Jeanette said. "My father says that a man looks at his son and wants him to do the things he had hoped to do in life. If anything gets in the way, it makes it hard. Girls, I guess, don't have to be so ambitious."

"But fathers can't understand very well," David said. Then he explained himself. "My dad is real great. I've seen him go through a lot, and I know he left South Town mostly for me—and for Betty Jane. But he can't understand that this was mostly my own fault. He kind of blames himself for me getting in trouble."

"How in the world does he figure that out?"

"Well, mostly because of where we live. You know how it is—east side, slum, tenants. He kind of figures if we had been living in a good part of town, and owning, then I would have had better friends and all."

"Like Buck Taylor, maybe?"

"Well, you know what I mean."

"Like Jeanette Lenoir, hunh?"

"You're twisting me up now. I mean, he means not like Hap and Head. Anyway, he's anxious to move now. When we first came he used to go out, he and my mother, every Saturday, all day long, looking at houses. Always the kind he wanted were too high, or else they weren't for sale to colored. But he keeps looking, him and Ma."

On Saturday when David awoke, it was snowing hard. He had wanted to sleep late, but that was impossible in the living room. Betty Jane was already up, begging him to get dressed and go outside with her.

"A person would think you'd never seen snow before," he said, laughing.

He looked out the window and saw that the snow was piling up fast. He was doubly glad it was Saturday for now maybe he'd have a chance to earn some money by shoveling snow. The weather was certainly different from South Town, he thought.

When he went into the kitchen for breakfast, Betty Jane was already in her ski pants and jacket, determined to build a snowman. His mother and father were also dressed.

"We're supposed to go look at some houses," Mr. Williams said. "We have to be at Mr. Taylor's office at nine o'clock."

As soon as David's case was dismissed, Mr. Taylor had resumed his role of real-estate broker. He knew that the Williams family were more than willing to buy.

"I don't see how anybody can drive in this weather," Mrs. Williams fretted.

"In this part of the country, business doesn't wait on a little snow," Mr. Williams told her. "Besides, today is the one day I can get out, and I guess the sellers will sure be home, and we'll have a good chance to see how well the heating system works. We just have to get an early start."

While they ate breakfast, David announced that he planned to borrow a snow shovel from the man who cleaned the halls and fired the furnace. Then he would go over to Stanton Park, a residential section on the other side of town, and look for work.

"Why don't you buy a shovel?" his father asked. "You can look at it this way—you're going to work, and the snow shovel is your tool. It's like a business; the tools are the investment. Tell you what I'll do." Mr. Williams took out his billfold. "Looks like you want a partner in this business. Let me make an investment. Say I furnish the tools and you pay me. Let's see—you cut me in for one fourth of the profits."

"That's too much, Ed," Mrs. Williams protested.

They finally agreed that David would borrow the money and when he had paid it back, the shovel would be his.

"Looks like," Mr. Williams spoke with an air of injured pride, "if I'm taking all the risk I should get something for a profit."

Betty Jane decided to look at houses, too, so they all left in the car together, Mr. Williams at the wheel. It was cold, and the snow was now more than a foot deep. Already people were out with shovels, and in the streets, plows scraped and clanked as they pushed the snow into neat piles.

David got out of the car on Main Street and watched as it merged with the slow-moving traffic going south. At the first hardware store he stopped and bought a shovel with a stout handle.

He found work long before he reached Stanton Park.

A stout woman, red-faced and unhappy in her efforts to clear her sidewalk, asked him if he wanted to do it. He said he would for a dollar, and he was hired. It took him less than half an hour, and he cleared a front path as wide as the paved sidewalk. He was surprised when the woman answered his ring with a pleased smile and gave him an extra quarter.

The snow shovel on his shoulder, he again started walking. In the next block another woman called to him from her front door. Again he quoted his price, and there was no objection. When he was through, she directed him to her neighbor's. He was kept so busy at a dollar a job, with frequent tips, that he began to wonder what it would be like in more prosperous Stanton Park. By one o'clock he had earned more than ten dollars. In spite of the cold, he was sweating from his exertions, and he had worked up a big appetite. He was not sure how he would be received in a public eating place in a white neighborhood, but he was so hungry that he decided to take a chance and entered an unassuming-looking snack bar.

The place was not full, but there was no empty stool at the counter which was not next to one occupied by a white customer. David figured he had to be careful. He did not want to be told that his "kind" was not welcome, as he knew happened, nor did he want to hear the embarrassing words, "We don't solicit colored trade here."

With his back to the counter, he carefully propped his snow shovel against the wall. Turning, he was soon aware that no one was watching him. He moved quickly to a stool between two other customers. Out of the corner of his eye, he saw that one was dressed in a Mackinaw and cap, the other in business clothes. Neither of them said a word. Soon the waiter asked him for his order.

"Two hamburgers, with everything on them, and milk to drink," David said. When the steaming sandwiches came, the man in the Mackinaw shoved the catsup bottle closer to David, a gesture more satisfying to David than the food he so hungrily gulped down.

The man finished his lunch and left, and another white customer took his place. When the waiter served him a hamburger, David reached for the catsup bottle and offered it to him.

"Thanks," the new customer said briefly.

David wished he had remembered to thank the man in the Mackinaw.

The wind was blowing when he went out, but the sun was shining. He had decided not to go all the way to Stanton Park. Nearby, not far from the business section, there were still walks to be cleared. In the first block, all but one walk was already shoveled, but in the next were several needing work. No one was home at the first house he tried. At the second an anxious elderly lady told him she guessed her son would come do the shoveling, but at the third house he was given a job. He had two more jobs in that block, one at the home of a girl from Central High who recognized him. When he was through, the girl's mother generously handed him two dollars and asked him to come back the next time it snowed.

In the next block he was surprised to come upon Mike O'Connor. Mike, bareheaded, was shoveling snow in an old pair of army pants and a blue ski parka. He greeted David with a wide grin. Ever since the first day at Central, in spite of his distrust of white people, David would have been forced to admit that Mike must be placed among the special exceptions: Mike was a "good guy."

"How're you doing, Dave?" he asked. "Making any money?"

"I've been doing well," David replied. "But I've been at it all day. One or two more jobs and I'll be ready to quit." He brushed the snow off his mittens.

"Well, that's just about what I was going to do. Say, why don't we go partners? I just started this job. It'll be a lot easier for both of us, working together, and we'll just go fifty-fifty. O.K.?"

David noticed that Mike was making only a narrow path, not trying to clear the whole sidewalk. He had done the porch steps the same way.

"I don't know if I've been charging as much as I should," Mike said, pausing to lean on his shovel handle. "When I started out, most people kicked at my prices. They want a man to work his heart out for free. I just passed up some of them who wanted to put up an argument. Later I did lower my price some."

David had been wondering about Mike's prices. "What are you getting for a job like this one?" he asked.

"I'm just getting two dollars." Mike seemed apologetic. "That all right with you?"

"That's all right. Sure, it's all right with me." In fact, David was thinking, it was high, especially considering the narrow path Mike made.

"I was asking for three on a job like this, but folks kicked so." Mike was bending again to his work. "Next job we can ask for three if you want."

David did not confess that he had been asking only a dollar. It was not easy to work and talk. Later, they took on several more jobs at two dollars and one corner job for five. By that time, it was getting dark, and they agreed that they had worked enough for one day.

"Hope it snows again tonight," Mike said. "How about us getting together again tomorrow? With a partner you can both do better. Don't you think so?"

He asked David where he lived, and David gave him his address, hoping that Mike would not know it was in a block of shabby flats.

"Say, that's not far from my place!" Mike seemed genuinely pleased. "If it snows, we can get out early. Prices are higher on Sunday—holiday, you know—and lots of men don't want to shovel snow, especially if they did it already on Saturday. They'll be laid up with aching backs. Man, we'll make a killing."

They were walking eastward. Mike did most of the talking, and David laughed at his wisecracks. He was thinking, too.

Today they had worked as partners, and Mike had proposed that they continue to work that way. Mike was white. He was a big football hero, and one of the most popular students at Central High, yet he lived on the east side, not far from where David lived.

David remembered the warnings he had heard. You can't trust them, Alonzo and the others had said. Down South you know white folks are against you and they're honest about it, while here they say everybody's equal, but they don't mean it. They may smile to your face but they'll laugh and knife you behind your back.

Mike was talking about his family.

"You know we always have beans for dinner Saturday night," he said. "I always know what it's to be for Saturday night—beans! My mother says it's her Boston upbringing, but my old man makes cracks about it, says it was her Boston downfall when she met him. But I like beans, you know, the way she cooks them—real old-fashioned, I guess."

David laughed. "I like 'em, too," he admitted. "We eat them with rice."

Along the edges of Main Street, only a little less busy after the storm than in good weather, the snow was in high piles like little mountain ranges. They were soon out of the business district. On Fourth Street the walking became more hazardous, because few paths had been cleared and they moved along in single file.

"Look, I live just around the next corner," Mike said.

"Why don't you stop by and have beans with me?"

David hesitated. He was not at all sure why this white boy, friendly as he seemed, would want to invite him to his home to eat with members of his family. He decided against it.

"Oh, your folks wouldn't be expecting me. It wouldn't be right," he demurred.

"It'll be all right," Mike insisted. "We always have plenty. Have to eat up the beans all day Sunday. What a load of beans my mom puts out! Course, we got plenty people there to eat them," Mike ran on. "I guess you never saw a family with so many kids. How many brothers and sisters have you got?"

"Just one sister. She's ten."

"See what I mean? I have three brothers and three sisters. Maybe that's the real reason we eat beans every Saturday night. Here's my corner." He stopped and faced David. "Come on," he urged. "I tell you it'll be O.K. with the folks. They'll be glad to meet you."

David did not want to seem stubborn. "I'll stop by just to see where you live," he said. "If it snows tonight, I'll come by for you in the morning."

Inwardly he wanted very much to see how Mike's family lived.

The houses now were neither large nor well kept, and the neighborhood looked very much like David's. Nondescript buildings stood close to the sidewalk, as though they wished to crowd out any space where, in winter, white snow might blanket city dirt or, in summer, grass or flowers might grow. If Mike O'Connor lived here,

David thought, the white students at Central must know it; yet the football team had chosen him captain. Maybe living on the east side was not so bad after all. And somehow David knew that his being colored did not matter to Mike.

In front of Mike's house the sidewalk and the path to the porch steps had been neatly shoveled. Mike said that his younger brothers must have done it, and that he guessed his father had checked to make sure it was cleared properly. On the front porch they stamped the snow off their galoshes; as they bent to remove them, the door opened and a boy rushed out. He was about eight years old and dressed in dungarees.

"Hey, Mike, how much money did you make?" he demanded loudly. Without waiting for an answer, he ran back into the house, shouting that Mike was home and that he had brought company. The other children hurried to the porch and filled the front hall as Mike led David indoors.

That was the beginning of David's welcome. No one said to him the words, "You are welcome, David Williams," but he knew he was. Mike proved to be the oldest of the children. His younger brothers, ages twelve and fourteen, had been out shoveling snow, too, and had earned enough to make them happy. They had to tell Mike all about their successes and failures and hard work. The sisters, to whom Mike formally introduced David, were less noisy, but they added to the pleasant confusion with their chatter and their laughter.

Mike took David through the house into the kitchen, which was large and brightly lighted. It looked clean, but it needed paint, and the gas range was the same old-fashioned kind that the Williamses had found in the flat they rented.

Mike's mother invited David to sit down and have dinner with her son. "We've plenty to eat, such as it is," she said.

"Thank you, ma'am," David replied quickly. "Thank you, but I know the folks are looking for me at home. Probably worried. Thank you very much, but I guess I better be getting on home."

He told Mike that if it snowed again that night he would be there at nine the next morning. Then he said good-bye and started home.

When David reached home, full of a new excitement, he found it was quite a while before he had a chance to tell about his day. Betty Jane met him at the door, almost jumping in her eagerness to give him the news. Mr. Taylor had found a house for them! It was hard for her to keep her voice down, and Mrs. Williams kept trying to quiet her because Mr. Williams was lying down with a bad headache.

"Wait till you see that bathroom!" Betty Jane exclaimed as she followed David into the kitchen. "Tile all over just like at school and a shower! And in my own room there's a clothes closet and in your room, too, and all the closets have lights in them. And, you know what? In Ma's and Pa's room the light comes on in the closet as soon as you open the door, and their room is bigger, bigger than two rooms here."

David saw that his mother shared Betty Jane's enthusiasm but that she was trying to be realistic, too.

"Don't go on so," she said, laughing. "We haven't got the house yet. You don't just look at a house and buy it as if it was a loaf of bread."

While she set David's dinner on the kitchen table, she

told him more about the house. It was on the west side, not in Stanton Park, but in a very nice section where all the houses had wide front yards.

David's plate held beans surrounded by frankfurters and a pile of fried potatoes. As he thanked God for his food, he remembered his own blessing, and when he looked up, he told his mother about his good fortune with the snow shovel.

"I don't even know how much I made," he said. "I'm going to count it after I put this dinner to bed. And, you know, I ran into Mike O'Connor—he's captain of the foot-ball team—and we started working partners. I saw his house. He lives not far from here, on the east side, and his folks were real nice. Well, maybe they're not poor, but they don't live so different . . . and for supper tonight they had beans, too, and they invited me to eat."

"They're white people?" Mrs. Williams asked.

"Yes, but—" David did not know how to put it. "They made me welcome. I figured maybe they didn't really mean it, and if I had sat down there, maybe they wouldn't like it. I don't know."

"Anyway, David"—his mother passed behind his chair and laid a hand on his shoulder—"you knew you had a good dinner waiting for you here, and our house may not be as fine as his, but it's home. And soon we'll be having a better one, and you'll invite him over to have dinner with you."

"No, Ma!" David shook his head. "His house wasn't fine. The things there weren't any better than ours, and the street, Fourth Street, is just about the same as Sixth Street. I don't even know that I'd want to invite him into the kind of house you all are talking about."

"Wait till you see it," Betty Jane interrupted excitedly. "You will then. You wouldn't be ashamed to bring anybody there."

"That's just it. I wouldn't be ashamed, but maybe he would. Maybe Mike—and he's a real nice guy, and we're going to be partners in snow-shoveling—but maybe in a house like that, Mike would think kind of that it would be too good for colored people, or especially newcomers from the South."

"But it will be our home, and I don't think your friend, especially if he's as decent as you say, would be like that. That would be showing jealousy," Mrs. Williams said.

"Not jealousy—" David was having trouble explaining. He began again. "Now like in shoveling snow today. Do you know the prices he was charging people, and they were paying? His prices were much higher than mine, and he wasn't even giving a good job. He probably made twice as much as I did. He wouldn't have cause to be jealous."

"How much did you make?" Betty Jane demanded. "Why don't you count it?"

David pushed his empty plate aside and counted his earnings. With the bills and the loose silver, he had more than twenty-six dollars. Even after he paid for the shovel, he would have made a profit of more than twenty dollars.

They had forgotten to keep their voices low, and Mrs. Williams was sorry to see her husband coming out of the bedroom in his bathrobe. His tired face showed deep lines. He hadn't slept; the aspirin had done no good, he admitted in response to her questions. He tried to smile his encouragement when David told him about his work and about his hope to earn even more money with Mike as partner.

"That's real good," he said. "It's an ill wind that blows nobody good, and this snow sure gives you a chance to make money. If this keeps up, we will be able to buy that house."

"Are we going to get it?" Betty Jane asked eagerly. "Are you going to buy that house, Pa?"

Mr. Williams did not answer immediately. Silently he watched while his wife poured a stream of hot, fragrant coffee into his cup. He spooned sugar into it and slowly added evaporated milk until the coffee lightened to just the right shade.

"There's a lot to buying a house," he finally said. "It's not as simple here as it was in South Town."

"How about the price?" David asked. "Have you got the money?"

"You don't have to have so much money to start buying. We've got enough for down payment, and the broker figures the monthly payments will be just about the same as a week's wages, and that's supposed to be good. We might have to go into more debt for furniture." He looked around the kitchen. "I don't think your ma would be happy without a modern stove and maybe living-room stuff, and we'd have to buy lots of other things."

"Do you think maybe some other house, maybe one not quite so fine, would do?" David asked.

"It's on the west side," Betty exclaimed. "That's where we want to live. That's where you said."

"Well," Mr. Williams said, "it's what we can get, and

for the money I know it's a bargain. It's just the special way things are right now and in that block."

"What is it?" David half guessed what the answer would be. "What is the special way things are?"

"The neighborhood is changing," his father answered. "One colored family bought in the block, and so white owners there are anxious to sell, even at a loss. The broker says this house is priced about three thousand dollars too low, and the owner will take just about any terms."

David thought a while. He remembered how many times his father had met only disappointment in his efforts to find somewhere for them to live at a price they could afford. He had heard friends say that it was practically impossible for colored people to buy a house at the advertised prices and terms quoted in the paper. He knew that the Taylors and the Lenoirs and many other colored families lived on the west side, and probably most of them had bought their houses from white people who were moving out because the neighborhood was changing.

"I think it's dirty," he said finally.

"You may be right," Mr. Williams said. "But this is one time race prejudice works in our favor."

"I know what you mean, son," Mrs. Williams put in. "And I feel the same way. I'd rather we could just buy with our means the right kind of place at a decent price."

"Isn't there a decent house in one of the neighborhoods where colored people already live?" David asked.

"What few there are for sale are priced too high." His father was shaking his head. "It looks like this is the best way to get out of this neighborhood. I want you and Betty

Jane to have better friends than you're finding."

David knew what his father meant. Still he wondered if moving into a big house in a white neighborhood was going to solve anything. He doubted it. Betty Jane was not sure either.

"I like the kids here and in school," she insisted. "They're not so bad. Still I'd like to live in that fine house we saw today." She paused and then asked, "I guess I couldn't keep going to Tenth Street School, could I?"

"No," Mrs. Williams replied. "You'd be going to school on the other side of town. That would be part of it. You'd soon make new friends."

They talked for a long time. At his father's suggestion, David got paper and pencils, and they made a list of the furniture they'd need. They calculated the monthly payments and the interest on the mortgage. While they discussed the prospects, Mrs. Williams put up the ironing board and pressed the dress Betty Jane would wear to Sunday school the next day.

At last they went to bed, David very much hoping that it would have snowed by the next morning. He had written down the address of the house they had talked about, and that, he decided, would be his first call for a snow-shoveling job.

TWELVE

IT HAD NOT SNOWED BY THE NEXT MORNING. In fact, there was very little snow that whole winter, and when it came, it was not on weekends. The partnership of Williams and O'Connor did not flourish. The two boys saw each other in the halls at school. Mike was always friendly, but as they had no classes together, they had little in common. Mike, a senior, was to graduate in June, and he complained about the necessity to study.

Mr. and Mrs. Williams, with David and Betty Jane helping, reached their decision. They bought the house, taking title and moving in on the first day of March. David found the two-story brick house every bit as impressive as Betty Jane had claimed, and he was happy to have a room of his own once again.

Mr. Williams, however, found that new furniture was much more expensive than he had anticipated. The sales people were very persuasive, and they made the credit terms sound easy. When they learned that he was working at the Foundation plant and that he was buying a house, they tried to convince him that real economy lay in purchasing what they called quality merchandise.

"You know there's only two kinds of furniture," one dealer told Mrs. Williams, trying to flatter her. "There's good furniture and then there's cheap furniture. Now we got the cheap stuff, too, but I can see you people know quality, and you probably wouldn't have the junk in your house that ignorant people buy."

"What we'll have to do," Mr. Williams said to his wife, "is try to get settled once and for all. You've got to have a place to invite your friends—the Lenoirs and people like them. And I don't want the kids to be ashamed, and not wanting other kids to see how we live."

Before they came to North Town, his family had lived about as well as any other colored family in the community. A man shouldn't let his standards fall, he felt. But when the bills were totaled, they showed scarcely any margin for living, and he worried. His headaches came more frequently, and they were more intense.

From Sixth Street, David had been close enough to walk to school, or, if he rode, to take only one bus. But now from West Twenty-fourth, after taking one bus downtown, he had to transfer to a second. With the coming of warmer weather, he often walked all the way. In the afternoon he really preferred to walk.

Jeanette lived nearby, and they usually walked together. They found they had many things to talk about. They were both ambitious, for they had grown up with parents who had encouraged them to acquire as much education as possible and thereby to make something of themselves. Jeanette told him about her home in New Orleans, and he told her the story of his family's trouble in the South.

David looked forward to the long walks, and he often went out of his way to take Jeanette to her door. If Mrs. Lenoir saw him, she would invite him in for a glass of milk and some pie or a piece of cake. He always said he shouldn't stop, but he always did.

One afternoon early in May they had walked more slowly than usual and were late, though David knew his mother had expected him earlier to help her set out some flowers. They were arguing, rather giddily, about the color of flowers, Jeanette insisting that more often than not they were yellow. David was trying to prove her wrong, but all they had seen on the way home were daffodils and bushes of forsythia.

As they approached her house, David was laughing for Jeanette had pointed out that there were dandelions blooming on her lawn. Then the front door flew open and Mrs. Lenoir, barely stopping to smile, called to him. "Your mother phoned, David. They want you at home right away." His father, she added, had become sick at the plant and been taken to the county hospital.

David ran most of the six blocks home. His heart pounding, he scarcely slowed for the traffic when he crossed Washington Boulevard. He knew if his father was so sick that they had taken him to the hospital, it must be serious. If it were not serious, they would have brought him home. He thought that it might have something to do with the headaches. Again he wished that Pa had gone to a doctor.

As he approached home, he felt something like surprise, surprise to see the house sitting there so impassively, the white posts of the wide porch still slim and clean-lined and dignified as though nothing had happened. He remembered that his father had said it would be nice to sit on that porch on the warm summer evenings. Fear clutched at David's throat as he turned and crossed the lawn toward the steps. Betty Jane was there on the porch to meet him.

"Where have you been, Dave?" she called, frantic with impatience. "We've been waiting and waiting! Pa's been taken to the hospital. Ma didn't know how to get there, and she had to wait for you. Do you know what bus we take?"

David had his own questions to ask, but Betty Jane did not know the answers. Inside the house, Mrs. Williams, already wearing her hat and coat, was coming down the stairs. She took David's arm.

"Son! We've been waiting for you. Why were you so long? I don't know . . . I don't know . . ." She was clinging to him.

David did not say that everything would be all right. He could not say it. He did not know. When Betty Jane spoke and took her mother's hand, he found a momentary course of action.

"Ma," Betty Jane pleaded, "Ma, we have to go to him."

"I don't think we ought to fool with buses," David said. "We'll have to get a taxi."

He drew away from his mother and went to the telephone. After the Yellow Cab office promised to send a taxi, he announced there was nothing now to do but wait.

"Yes," Mrs. Williams admitted with a sigh, "we'll have to wait. Nothing else we can do now." She picked up her purse from the chair where she had dropped it and reached into it for a handkerchief with which to wipe her eyes.

David, seeing his mother calmer, went to the kitchen. There was nothing there he wanted, but he turned on the water and let it run hard, while he stood leaning against the sink. He covered his mouth with his hand. He was not ashamed to be crying, but he didn't want his sister to hear him. He was afraid. He tried not to think about something serious happening to his father. Instead, he tried to think of some way he could help, but he could find none; rather, he felt it was all his fault. His arrest and all that dirty business had put a terrible extra strain on his father and made his headaches more severe. Then they had moved with too much debt and worry into a better neighborhood. His father had sacrificed too much.

"O God," he prayed. "Please don't let anything happen to him."

He struggled to get control of himself, and when his breathing returned to normal, he splashed water on his face and dried it on a paper towel.

"Got to go," he said to himself resolutely.

While they waited for the taxi to come, Mrs. Williams told David as much as she knew. Two telephone calls had come; the first from Andy Crutchfield who said that Ed had felt sick and gone to the hospital and that she shouldn't be upset if he didn't get home on time. The second call was from a nurse on the staff at the plant. This time she was told that Mr. Williams had been taken to the hospital by ambulance, after collapsing on the job. He was unconscious; his exact condition was not known; but it was suggested that she might want to go to the hospital.

David knew one word for a sudden collapse. He hesitated to use it, and when he did, he tried to have confidence in what he said, "Pa's not old enough to have a stroke."

THIRTEEN

DAVID WAS RIGHT. IT WAS NOT A STROKE. It was several hours before they knew this, however, and even when they did, the news brought no relief. First, while David and Betty Jane sat patiently in the waiting room, Mrs. Williams had to be interviewed by the admissions office. There she was asked to sign several forms, and when she hesitated, the interviewer told her that someone had to authorize the necessary treatment and, since it was clear that the patient was unable to do so, it was up to his wife, the next of kin. Still hesitating, Mrs. Williams took up the pen. She said she supposed it was all right; only she wished she had someone to advise her.

"It is all right, Mrs. Williams," the interviewer told her, and reaching over, she patted her hand. "It really is. I don't know the details on this case, but I know that you will want the doctors to do whatever is necessary. They will do their best."

"Yes, yes." Mrs. Williams signed quickly without reading the papers. "I know. Whatever is necessary."

"This form"—the woman pointed to it as she spoke—"authorizes diagnosis and treatment including surgery. This one acknowledges financial responsibility, meaning beyond whatever the insurance pays. And this one releases the hospital from liability for personal property and also authorizes us to deal with you as responsible next of kin. You'll be going up to Critical on the second floor. The doctor there may be able to tell you something more, and perhaps he will want to ask about the patient's medical history. I do hope your husband will be better soon."

To David and Betty Jane, their mother's interview seemed endless. Actually they could see by a clock on the wall that it was not long. But the hands moved slowly. It was after five o'clock. The large waiting room was nearly empty. Across the lobby, David could see an arrow labeled "Cafeteria" pointing to the right, and he could hear the clatter of dishes and silverware. He was a little ashamed that he should be thinking of food, but he wondered what would happen if they walked into the cafeteria. Would they be turned away? He thought not, but maybe the colored people there always ate at certain tables.

Here in the county general hospital, as in the schools, there seemed to be no open segregation. He had already noticed other colored visitors and some colored nurses. He wondered if the doctors and nurses—white doctors and nurses, that is—treated colored patients as well as they did white patients. He had heard it said, though he hadn't wanted to believe it, that the doctors experimented on colored people. But Jeanette had told him it was not so, and he believed most of what Jeanette said. Still, he was unsure of many things. He wouldn't always be so unsure, he resolved. Someday he would know the answers. He would learn for himself about hospitals where doctors who were white treated and prescribed for colored men and colored women, and operated on them, laying open their bodies, cutting through the dark skin, and peering into their insides where there were no race problems. He thought of the white veteran who had said, "On the battle-field the black soldiers had guts the same color as mine!"

Finally his mother was through with her interview, and they took the elevator to the second floor. The elevator operator, as though she knew their problem, told them to go down the corridor to the right. There a nurse greeted them. She was stout and past middle age; her cap carried four parallel black stripes. And she was colored. It was easy to talk to her, and after the first few words, some of the fear left Mrs. Williams's face and voice, and David stopped wondering whether his father would be kindly treated.

The nurse reported that Mr. Williams's had been in a coma when he was brought in, that his condition hadn't changed, and that there was still uncertainty about the diagnosis. He had been examined by a specialist, who wanted more information about his medical history.

Mrs. Williams quickly described the headaches from which her husband suffered, and the nurse thought that they might be important. But when Mrs. Williams went on to say how sorry she was that she had not made her husband go to a doctor for treatment, the nurse shook her head.

"At a time like this," she said, "whatever happens or however bad it looks, we have to look forward, not back. There are things to do now. We can't dwell on the things that we left undone. In this place we learn that.

"Now!" She became more businesslike. "The doctor will be seeing you, and you will want to answer all his questions. Tell him all about your husband's health and anything you feel is important. You just sit down over there, honey. Let the boy go get you some coffee. There's a machine down the hall. And don't you worry. Pray, but don't worry."

They did not have long to wait. A doctor in a white hospital coat was seated beside his mother when David returned, with a paper cup of hot coffee. He was a thin-faced man of about sixty with wispy blond hair. Betty Jane was standing nearby. As David hesitated, the doctor motioned to him and said to Mrs. Williams, speaking abruptly and with a heavy European accent, "Drink your coffee. Drink your coffee."

When he found out about the beating Mr. Williams had undergone in South Town, he wanted to know exactly how long ago it had occurred and whether there had been much physical injury at the time. He asked what medical treatment had been prescribed, and Mrs. Williams told him that their doctor, Dr. Anderson, seemed to have done the right things, for recovery had been swift.

"X-rays? What about X-rays?" the doctor asked. "I would see those X-rays from that time. Then with those we make now, maybe we see something."

"Oh, I don't think so." Mrs. Williams shook her head and looked at David for confirmation. "No, I'm sure he didn't take any X-rays. You see that was in the country and in the South. They don't have X-rays there. No hospitals."

"So! So!" The doctor nodded. He was silent for a moment. "So!" he said again. "Now after? When does he have pains before today?"

Mrs. Williams told him everything she could, as accurately as she could. Often she glanced at David when she was not certain, and when she did, the doctor looked at David, too.

Finally, the doctor spoke to him. "What you think, young man?" he asked. "You know something more?"

"Oh, no, sir." David was surprised that he should be asked, but since the doctor had inquired he thought he should tell him what he was thinking. "Only something I did notice. Mostly the pains would come when he was worried about something. Seems like lately he's had much to worry about."

"So! So!" The doctor seemed to feel it might be important. "Is right!" He stood and looked down at Mrs. Williams, and then at David and Betty Jane.

"To worry is not good," he said. "Now the patient is not worrying He is waiting. Just waiting. Maybe we will do something. His heart is not bad. His respiration is good. In the pictures we made already, we do not see much. Now you tell me about damage less than one year ago. We will take more pictures and maybe we see more this time. Then maybe we know more of what we must do."

Mrs. Williams had risen. She looked very small beside the tall doctor.

"He will be all right? Won't he, doctor?" she asked.

"Good lady, I wish I could say yes. Now, I do not know. We cannot yet say what is the trouble. In one hour, maybe two, we will know more. His condition, as you know, is serious. He is on critical list. There is nothing for you to do here now. You should go home, maybe give your children some dinner."

"I can't go, doctor!"

"We don't want to eat!" David and Betty Jane said together.

"So! He is a good man. We are going to do everything we can for him." The doctor repeated, "Everything!"

They knew that they could not leave. They would have to wait at the hospital. There was nothing they could do to help. They had told the doctor everything they knew.

If someone had asked what they were waiting for, they could not have said. But really they were waiting for something very important. They were waiting for news— in hope, in desperate hope, that the news would be good; in heartaching fear that it would be bad.

When his mother asked if David and Betty Jane did not want to get something to eat, David told her about the cafeteria on the first floor, but she refused to leave and David would not go without her. Instead, he and Betty Jane walked down the hall to the coffee machine. Feeding two dimes into it and punching a different button, they got paper cups of hot chocolate. From another machine, they bought small packages of cookies and candy bars. With this, they slaked their hunger.

While they were nibbling their cookies, Andy

Crutchfield appeared. With him was their pastor, the Reverend Mr. Hayes, from the First Baptist Church. Andy Crutchfield offered to help in any way he could.

"I know it don't sound right to say don't worry, Mrs. Williams," he said. "But this is what I mean: don't worry about nothing like money or the job or getting things done. Ed Williams going to have the best care they can give. They got some of the best doctors in the country right here. They know what to do, and what it costs don't matter 'cause what the insurance don't pay we going make up, anyway.

"Now," he went on. "I ain't even seen her yet 'cause I came on here only stopping by to pick up Reverend, so I ain't seen my wife yet, but she's going cook up some dinner, and when you all are home, she going run over and do whatever you want as long as you need her. So that part you don't have to worry about. Course about Ed, well, we all going be praying, and I guess I can't say don't worry, but I say you won't be worrying alone. We with you."

The Reverend Mr. Hayes pledged the assistance of his church. Then sitting down beside Mrs. Williams, he closed his eyes and, almost inaudibly, he prayed. Before leaving, he gave Mrs. Williams his card with his telephone number, and asked her to let him know about her husband's progress. With the card he handed her a folded five-dollar bill. She might be able to find a use for it, he said, since these things almost always called for more cash than you figured on.

After they had gone, David remembered that Mrs. Lenoir had asked him to telephone her. He had seen a booth on the main floor, and, telling his mother what he wanted to do, he ran down the stairway, rather than wait for the elevator. As he slid into the seat of the telephone booth and pulled the door shut behind him, he heard his name. Jeanette was coming toward him, and behind her was her father.

"We've been trying to see you. They wouldn't let us go upstairs," she explained. "How's your father?"

David told them all he knew, repeating what the nurse and the doctor had said. Then he added that he felt the hospital was doing everything it could and that he trusted the doctor.

"And your mother?" Jeanette asked.

"Ma? Ma is swell. She can really take it," David said. "Betty Jane, she's just a kid. She . . . she . . . she's O.K., I guess."

"Is there anything we can do?" Mr. Lenoir asked. "Should we notify anybody in South Town? We could send telegrams or telephone, if you liked."

"No. No, sir." David was emphatic. "I don't think we should do that."

In David's native community, telegrams were frightening; too often they brought the sad news of death. Many families in South Town did not have their own telephone, and even now that the Williams family were in North Town, they were not used to making long-distance calls.

There was nothing for the Lenoirs to do, but David thanked them for coming and told them that he knew his mother would feel better for knowing that they had been there. He promised that he would telephone them as soon as he had more news.

When the news did come, it was not good.

At last the doctor returned, accompanied by a tall,

young man. A careful examination of a large number of X-rays, he reported, showed that Mr. Williams's skull had previously been fractured. The break had mended, but the thin layer of tissue that lay between the skull and the brain had thickened. In the passing months the thickening had increased, causing more and more pressure. It was this that had caused the intense headaches and finally his collapse. The pressure could be relieved only by an operation.

"Dr. Osborne is a highly competent surgeon," he said with a gesture toward the tall young man beside him. "He is a specialist in brain surgery. He will operate."

"When? When will it be?" Mrs. Williams's voice shook.

"We will not be able to operate until tomorrow morning." Dr. Osborne spoke for the first time. "We're making tests, and he will have to have some treatment." Then he spoke of certain medicines and of intravenous feeding. "Of course, we can't say at this time what the possibilities are, but we will be doing our best."

Mrs. Williams looked at her son and then at her daughter. "We know you will," she said. "We believe you." She put an arm around Betty Jane and added, "We will be praying."

Dr. Osborne suggested that they go home and have supper and try to get some rest. He promised to talk to them again in the morning.

It was past midnight when they wearily took the elevator downstairs. There they found Andy Crutchfield waiting for news and to help in any way he could. He drove them to his own house where Mrs. Crutchfield had dinner waiting for them. She had prepared fried chicken, hot biscuits, and plenty of vegetables, though she apologized for the meal, saying that she hadn't really had time to fix anything nice.

In spite of their anxiety, they ate. David's well-known appetite was not at all diminished by worry.

After they finished, Mrs. Crutchfield insisted on going home with them. She had an overnight bag already packed, planning to stay as long as she was needed. "Guess Andy be glad enough to get shed of me for a while," she said.

No one believed what she said, and they all laughed. When Mrs. Williams protested that staying overnight was hardly necessary, Mrs. Crutchfield told her, "I know what you would do for me, or for any other one in trouble. Now I ain't saying you need me or I can do so much, but I want to be there anyway for what little I can do. Just don't pay me no mind. I won't be in your way."

She had a ham ready for baking and a shopping bag full of what she called "a few little things," when they got into the car.

After Mr. Crutchfield had taken the others home, he drove David over to the plant to get his father's car.

"I guess you know, son," he said very seriously, "this could be right bad." David nodded.

"Your daddy is a good man," Mr. Crutchfield went on. "He's seen you through to the place where you got good schooling, more than he ever had, lots more than me. Course I know you planned to graduate, and that's what he wanted, too. Well, if you can't stay in school and finish, don't feel too bad. You'll make it. You'll make it good. Same as I got your daddy in out to the plant I can get you in. He made a good record and they'll be glad to put his son to work, and they'll give you a chance to learn, get to be a skilled man. Pretty soon you might have to be the man of the house. You're big and strong. I guess that's what your daddy would want."

David realized the truth of what his family's best friend was saying. He was not unhappy for himself at the prospect. His father wanted him, perhaps even more than David did, to graduate from high school and go on to college. David knew that his father did not know, as David had come to realize, that there were countless hazards to block the precarious way through college, and that only the very smart and the very lucky could hope to enter medical school. He had learned that it was hard for any student, and he knew it was even harder for a colored boy. If it should be too bad for his father, he would indeed have to take his place as the man of the family. He would have to meet his responsibility.

In the parking lot at the plant the guards on the night shift knew Andy Crutchfield. They waved David through on Crutchfield's word, and he drove quickly home.

Mrs. Williams had been told to return to the hospital at nine in the morning. It was scarcely half past eight when she and her children arrived. In contrast to yesterday's quiet, the waiting room on the ground floor seemed a beehive of activity. Every seat was occupied. Mrs. Williams had to wait in line to get passes permitting them to take the elevator to the second floor. The line moved forward slowly.

Many people in the room appeared sick to David. Very few seemed to be visitors. Even the mothers with sick children looked as though they, too, should be under the care of a doctor. If he were a doctor, he thought, he would make a point of looking after the health of the family as well as of the patient confined to bed. If he were a doctor! he thought longingly.

Ahead of him, his mother gave their names and the name of her husband. After checking a card file, the attendant wrote a pass for three.

At the desk on the second floor, a uniformed attendant told them that Mr. Williams was resting comfortably in the post-operative room. She said she would check and let them know when he might be seen.

"Post-operative?" Mrs. Williams asked. "That means . . ."

"Yes. The patient went to surgery at 6:00 A.M." She looked at a chart. "He was there," she said, watching Mrs. Williams's reaction, "he was there more than two hours. You are his wife?" Mrs. Williams nodded. "Perhaps you'll be allowed to see him, but it will probably be some time before they know much about his condition. If you will be seated, I'll locate the doctor. He's expecting you."

They felt cheated. No one had said that the operation would take place so early. Yet, now that it was over, David realized that all of them, especially his mother, had been spared the pain of knowing that for two hours his father had been lying helpless, though unconscious surely and without pain, while surgeons cut into his head. Fearful visions suggested by scenes in movies and pictures in magazines and books swam before David's eyes. They had been just pictures then, but now as he connected them with his own father, active, strong, and close, they were horrible.

He put his arm around his mother and led her to a seat. She was weeping softly. Tears filled his own eyes, and he could not stop them.

It was here that the doctor with foreign accent came to them. He brought a chair and sat down, not to explain what had been done, but to express frank admiration for Dr. Osborne and those who had assisted him. He said with some hesitation that so far the operation had been successful. Mr. Williams's condition was satisfactory. The next several hours would tell—maybe twelve, maybe twenty-four. His reactions when the effects of anaesthesia wore off would be significant.

"Doctor," David asked, "could you tell us what the chances are for full recovery?"

"So! Young man, you want a percentage." The doctor shook his head. "We have no statistics. Never are two cases exactly the same. If you make me say figures, suppose we call it fifty per centum for physical recovery. Then we have something else again for that damage that the operation does not relieve. Sometimes—Must I say this?—sometimes there is left some paralysis or loss of function that cripples, and sometimes it is the mind.

"Only so much we can do," he said, hurrying on, knowing that his words were painful. "Some things we can do, and some he will do."

"You mean," Mrs. Williams asked, "you mean he will have to help himself?"

"More, lady, more. I mean more than that. It is not what he has to do, but what he can do. Is he a man of hope? That is not the same as being a man of strong will. And I think it is more. In my country, in the land I came from, I have seen good men destroyed, thousands of them. Men with strong will, I have seen them broken. In the pogroms, and in ghettos, and in concentration camp. But I have seen other people, who were weak and had no skill and nothing to fight back with but only hope. And somehow, I do not understand it, with hope some people will live when all we know of science and matter will say they should die.

"I am not sure," the doctor said. "Maybe hope is not the word I mean."

"I think I know." Mrs. Williams herself seemed to have gained courage from what the doctor had said. "I believe you mean faith."

"No. It is not faith, not faith like the Christians talk about. Hope is the word most near what I mean."

It was late that morning when they saw Mr. Williams. They were not prepared and the picture shocked them. David had gone downstairs to the cafeteria to bring up sandwiches. They were tired and uncomfortable. Other visitors had come and gone. They had seen a number of patients wheeled by in chairs or lying flat on tables with large rubber-tired wheels. So it was with David's father. An elevator door opened, and a male orderly in a white uniform called out for clearance as he pushed a table before him. A nurse walked close beside the patient, holding high a jar of amber-colored liquid from which a tube hung down and lost itself under the covers. As the group moved closer, Mrs. Williams sprang up with a little cry. Her husband's face—that part of it which showed beneath the bandages swathing his head—was very still.

His skin, usually darker than David's, was ashy gray as though it were heavily dusted with white powder.

"Keep clear, please!" the orderly called again.

At four o'clock the kindly colored nurse, whom they had met the day before, returned to duty. She checked the charts and told them that the anesthetic had worn off, but that the patient was being kept asleep under heavy sedation. He was being fed intravenously, and his condition showed no change. In her opinion it was too early to expect any change. She presumed that he would be kept asleep under drugs until the following day. She suggested that the family go home, and Mrs. Williams surprised David by agreeing.

Just before they left, the nurse led Mrs. Williams into the critical ward to stand beside her husband's bed. David and Betty Jane followed them to the door but they did not enter. The nurse was very casual, exchanging greetings in her normal voice with those patients who were able to talk. Going to Mr. Williams's bed, she straightened the covers and smoothed the sheet; then smiling broadly, she took the hand of Mrs. Williams and laid it gently across the lips of the sleeping man.

"You know," she said, "I think he's going to be all right. Seeing you and his kids, I figure he's got what it takes. Um-huhm! He's probably got it."

Mrs. Williams did not ask whether she meant hope or faith. Whichever it was, she too thought that her husband had it.

FOURTEEN

D R. MEYER, THE DOCTOR WHO HAD LIVED IN GHETTOS, suffered in pogroms, and survived in concentration camps, decided that his patient was a man who had hope. It took only a few days of observation and tests to determine that he had come through the operation without loss of physical function.

The question of his mental and emotional condition was less easy to answer. The nurses observed that he always seemed brighter when his wife was present, and while he was in a critical condition, they did not discourage her visits. When he was moved upstairs to the regular ward, his wife became subject to the limited visiting hours prescribed by hospital regulation.

David was out of school three days, Wednesday through Friday, and on Sunday he discussed with his mother the advisability of his staying out to work for the rest of the term. Mr. Crutchfield had already spoken to someone at the plant who had offered to hire the son of Ed Williams.

"Oh, no, David," Mrs. Williams protested. "We don't have to take you out of school. Not yet. I believe things will work out, and anyway we can make it somehow to the end of the semester."

Back in school on Monday, his homeroom teacher asked how his father was. When he told her that his father was still in the hospital and his condition still critical, she expressed her sympathy and promised him any help she could give. His other teachers remarked that they hoped he would be able to catch up on the work he had missed. In biology Miss Nichols told him to make up his experiments whenever he could in the lab. It would not have been difficult to copy someone's lab notes without doing the experiments, but she knew he would not take this easy way out.

At lunchtime he went to the cafeteria with Jeanette. When he told her that he must consider making changes in his plans, that he might have to go to work, she answered almost as his mother had. "Oh, David! Not now!" she said. "You're just getting adjusted. Why, this is no time to stop."

"But you don't understand," he said. "We really need the money."

All their savings had been put into the house, he explained, and they were still heavily in debt for the mortgage and the furniture, and now probably there'd be hospital and medical expenses. He wasn't sure, but he guessed that these last would be much more than any insurance payments would take care of. Jeanette listened closely but said nothing. Then he told her what Andy

Crutchfield had suggested. She had been frowning, not so much in annoyance as in thought. Now she smiled.

David had thought for a long time that Jeanette's smile was something wonderful. Now, to his surprise she seemed delighted, and he did not understand why.

"Of course," she exclaimed. "That's wonderful. Why, you could stay on the night shift until the end of the semester and then go on days—or maybe you wouldn't even want to. I didn't know you meant working like that. I thought you were talking about dropping out altogether."

"But I was," David started to say. Then he stopped for he realized she had offered a solution. "That is, at first I was thinking about it the other way. I know Mr. Crutchfield was figuring for a day job. He wouldn't know that my folks want me to go on through school as much as I do."

"No, he wouldn't, and the people at the plant wouldn't either, but that's all right."

"Every place my father has worked he's made good," David said proudly. "Last summer I worked in a shop where he used to work. It was rough, and the boss made trouble, but just the same, thinking about it now, they had a good feeling for my dad, and in their way they respected him."

"Everybody who knows Mr. Williams has to respect him" Jeanette agreed.

It was one week later that David started working at the Foundation plant. He was on the night shift, from four to midnight, and his starting pay was more than he had expected.

Mr. Crutchfield had not thoroughly approved of

David's plan to remain in school. He thought that David already had more education than a man needed. He could not encompass David's dream of going to college and becoming a doctor. He thought that such ideas were for white people, or for very rich colored people, certainly not for anyone within his own circle of friends.

On the job David was classified as a laborer. This he had anticipated. His duties were those of a janitor. He worked with a clean-up crew, all of whom were colored. The lead man, Smith, was settled, past middle age, of the same general outlook as Andy Crutchfield. Steady, reliable, and hard-working, he sought the same qualities in his crew and complained that they were hard to find. He said his men were lazy and inefficient, and he was tired of having to run behind them. He was suspicious of David until he learned he was Ed Williams's boy. After that, he was kinder to him. He gave David more work, but he "ran behind him" less. "Running behind a man," David learned, was Smith's concept of supervision.

If David did not like some of the details of his job, he did enjoy the chance to work and to bring home a man's pay. His daily schedule was soon readjusted. To save time he usually drove to school and then to the plant. His seventh period, the last in the school day, was free on three days, and on the other two, he was in biology lab for the sixth and seventh periods. His homeroom teacher helped him to get excused for the three free days and released "when necessary" from the lab, but he was expected to keep up with his schoolwork.

It was not too hard to do. He found that if he paid closer attention in class and spent more of his study time in the library and less in the noisy study hall, or worse in the halls, he could still turn in his written work and make fairly good recitations.

Friday night at the end of his first week of work, he came home to find his mother waiting for him as usual. During the week she had been sleeping in the early part of the evening and then getting up at midnight to prepare her son's supper.

"I don't see how you're going to stand it, son," she said. "You're not getting your rest, and eating sandwiches and cold food all day!"

"Never mind, Mother." David tried to reassure her. "It's not so bad, and look at this!" He drew a check from his shirt pocket and proudly displayed it. "That's just for a couple of days. More than I made in three weeks at home. Guess I can lose a little sleep for money like that."

"But your health! No amount of money would be worth breaking down your health."

"It's only for a few weeks, Ma. Then school is out." He scrubbed his hands at the kitchen sink while his mother explained that she hadn't had time to make hot biscuits. She had overslept, she said; he would have store-bought bread tonight for supper.

"How's Pa?" David asked, taking his place at the chrome kitchen table.

"He says he's fine. Wants to come home. Really, he's looking better, and the nurses tell me they've never seen such a good recovery." From a container, she poured milk into a glass for David.

"How about the other?" David deliberately busied himself with the liver and onions before him.

"They say it's too early to know really." Mrs. Williams sat down opposite her son. She sighed heavily. "They say that even after he comes home we might not know for a long time."

David had not seen his father since Sunday. At that time he had been fully conscious, awake, and apparently not in pain, but he was clearly not right mentally. He had not recognized either his son or his daughter.

It had been hardest on Betty Jane. She had cried, and David had had to take her out of the room. He had tried to comfort her, telling her that Pa was improving and that they should be thankful he was even alive after all he had gone through. He repeated to her the encouraging words of the doctors and nurses, yet, even while he said them, his arm tightly around his sister, he was trying desperately to believe them himself.

Now as he asked about "the other," Mrs. Williams knew full well what he meant.

She went to the stove and turned up the burner under the coffeepot. She waited there, not speaking, and when the coffee was percolating, she poured herself a cup and started back to the table.

David's plate was nearly empty. He drank the last of the milk in his glass.

"I think I'll have some coffee," he said.

"It might keep you awake," she objected, but she poured him out a cup.

"I'll sleep tonight," David said, smiling.

Seated again, she went on as though she had not been interrupted. "He's just like a little child, maybe five or six or maybe seven years old. It's hard to see him like that. It's like you would have been about the time you were starting school. If only I had gotten him to go to the doctor when we first came to North Town!"

"Ma, you can't blame yourself."

"I'm not blaming myself, but if I had only known!"

"It might not have been any different."

"Just like a little boy! He's glad to see me. He frets when I have to leave him. He calls me 'Maummy,' and when he talks about going home, I can tell it's not this house he means. It's home down South, the farm he grew up on."

"Have you heard from any of the folks?"

"Oh! I forgot." She left the table and got a letter off a table in the front hall. "There's a letter from your Aunt Mattie. She's coming."

The letter from his father's only sister was postmarked Richmond, Virginia, where she lived with her family. Ed Williams was the youngest of six children. After growing up on a farm in Pocohantas County, the members of the family had scattered. Only one brother remained at home. All the others had moved farther north.

When David finished reading the letter, he checked the dates of Aunt Mattie's visit.

"Why, this means Aunt Mattie will be here Sunday," he said. "That's just day after tomorrow."

"Tomorrow, really." Mrs. Williams smiled at the prospect. "It's already Saturday."

"She'll be able to visit Pa Sunday afternoon." He glanced at the letter again. "Of course, she doesn't know," he added. "Will you tell her?"

"Mattie's always been so understanding. I'll tell her. I think she'll be able to help. She and your father were very close."

David yawned and stretched. It was time to go to bed. He knew he would have to mow the lawn in the morning. He usually washed the car on Saturday, too, and did other chores around the house.

"Sleep late tomorrow," his mother said, reading his mind. "You need the rest. Betty Jane and I can manage. You get to bed now."

David said good night. His mother kissed him, standing on tiptoe because he never seemed to bend down quite enough. He went to bed, thinking that tomorrow, after cutting the grass, he would drive over to see Jeanette.

At seven thirty in the morning Mrs. Williams heard her son get up. She met him in the hall with his eyes half open.

"Why didn't somebody call me?" he asked sleepily.

His mother led him back to his room, and when he lay down, she pulled the covers over him. Then she went to the kitchen to warm some milk for him, but when she returned with it, he was sound asleep. He slept until six in the evening.

The school year drew to a close. The week of final examinations was quickly upon David, who prepared for it as best he could. The seniors were getting ready for their graduation. David caught a glimpse of Mike O'Connor hurrying in his cap and gown to the auditorium, where the senior class was rehearsing for commencement exercises. Later that afternoon as he was leaving the building, Mike hailed him. The two girls he had been talking to looked crestfallen as he left them to catch up with David. He fell in step beside him, and they walked toward the high school parking lot where David had the car.

"I bet you're glad this is your last week," David said, "and when you get out of here you'll be gladder still."

"It might not be as rosy as you think," Mike replied. "I'm beginning to see why they call it commencement."

To David's question about which college he planned to go to, Mike shook his head.

"I don't think I'll be going. I can't be hanging around any longer. I'm going to work. Anyway, I can't afford to go to college."

"But you're an athlete, Mike," David protested. "There's always talk about athletic scholarships. What about help like that?"

"I guess I really could swing it, if I wanted to. It's the folks. I've got my basic education now, and my dad's been plugging along, but we're a big family, you know. I think I ought to help. I'll just get me a job."

David was surprised, but he did not indicate it. "Guess I know what you mean. I'm working now. Night shift at Foundation."

"You are? Say, I was thinking about coming out there. Maybe you can get me on. I'll do anything. You know I can work," Mike said earnestly.

"Sure, but . . ." David was about to say that he had only started and had no way to get anybody a job, especially a white boy.

"Look," Mike said, "what I need now is work. They say the best way to get a job is to know somebody, right?

So I know you, Dave Williams, and we're already partners, remember?"

David remembered. He wished there were something more he could do to help Mike. Getting his own job had been perilous enough. Andy Crutchfield had been able to swing it only because of David's father.

Mike left him at the parking lot, calling as David drove away, "See what you can do for me!"

At the plant the day shift's time overlapped the night shift by an hour. In that hour David looked up Andy Crutchfield. Just maybe, he thought, the old man would use his influence because Mike was David's friend.

After assuring him that he was getting along fine at the plant and that his father was improving and would soon be home, David told him that a friend of his from Central was looking for a job. He asked whether Mr. Crutchfield would help him get placed.

"Good man, is he? High school graduate?" When David nodded, Andy Crutchfield seemed pleased. "I could use a man like that, might use him on my own crew, if he is willing and respectful."

That wasn't what David had intended. He wished that he had come right out and said it plainly at first. Then he wished that he had said nothing at all and that Mike had not asked him to help. All the men on Crutchfield's gang were colored. They were janitors. Their hopes for advancement were limited to chances for the job of lead man, like Crutchfield or Smith.

"Mr. Crutchfield," David explained, "I didn't mean on your crew. My friend is a white boy, but he's all right."

Mr. Crutchfield seemed to swell up with anger. "A white boy? A white boy? How come you got to look out for a white boy? Ain't you got troubles enough of your own? What he trying to do, get your job? I don't work no mixed crew. Don't want no white man with me. Besides any white boy can get his own job. Let him shift for hisself, I say. If he so poor he got to get you to help him, he trash anyway. I got nothing for a poor white man to do. Not nothing at all."

David started to back away.

"I say No!" Mr. Crutchfield was more and more vociferous. "I got nothing for him. I wouldn't give a poor white man a crust a bread if he starving or a drink of water if he burning in hell. I say No!" He moved suddenly toward David. "And I tell you another thing, you better get some sense and just cause you up North don't think you going look out for the white boys and they going look out for you. They ain't. I say No!"

David, shocked and embarrassed, hurried out of the room. He could hear Mr. Crutchfield scolding when he could no longer see him, and through the night he seemed to hear the echo of his storm as he swept shop floors and dusted offices and sloshed soapy water over the tile of toilet rooms, "I say No!"

On a bulletin board near the main gate was an announcement headed APPRENTICES. David had not read it before, but that night he looked it over carefully and made a note of what it said for Mike: "High school graduate or equivalent. Ages 17 to 24. Testing for aptitudes. Good character. Career-minded."

FIFTEEN

Ed Williams was discharged from the hospital on June fifteenth. It was a Tuesday, the day of biology finals. David missed the examination, but he knew Miss Nichols would let him take the exam later.

His father had done well. He was no longer confined to bed, and his incisions had healed so clearly that only small scars would be left. But he still thought as a child, and the things he remembered were of his boyhood. His questions showed he was puzzled. So many things had to be repeated. He had been delighted when his sister Mattie appeared, but he talked with her about their brothers as children, and the school they had attended. The Crutchfields had visited him each Sunday, but he remembered Andy only from his life in Pocohantas County. He recalled nothing of his job at the Foundation.

If anyone tried to make him remember, he was hurt. At times he spoke in anger. More often he was silent.

So they brought him home. He rode in the front seat beside David, enjoying the bounce of the soft seat, watching David's movements, at one time reaching out his own hand to rest on the steering wheel and smiling as David turned the wheel and the car responded. Nothing he said showed that he had a hidden impulse to take the wheel. He had nothing to say to his wife or his sister or Betty Jane, who were riding in back.

When they turned into their driveway, he asked where they were. When told it was his home he would not believe it, and although he got out of the car, he did not want to go inside the house. His sister took one arm and David the other while Mrs. Williams went ahead to unlock the door.

He stumbled as he went up the steps. David could feel him trembling and see that his face was wet with perspiration. They talked to him, easing his fears. He was coming home, to his own house to live with his own family. He would have good home-cooking. He would sleep in his own bed. Soon he would be felling fit as a fiddle.

They went through the motions, and they said the words, but they were not sure. They wanted very much to believe that within a matter of days or weeks or, even, months they would see him well again. They wanted to believe, but they were prepared to care for him if necessary for the rest of his life, and they were determined that no one should hurt or shame him.

After a few days they could tell that he was happy. He

enjoyed his house. He would go through the rooms, sliding his slippered feet along the hardwood floors. On the warm summer days and in the evenings, he sat contentedly on the porch. Often he would look about him as he leaned on the porch rail or put out his hand to open the door, and would smile and say softly, "This my house."

He had no idea of the financial problems with which his family was struggling. The total of the insurance benefits and David's earnings fell far short of meeting their bills.

Mr. Taylor went over the accounts with Mrs. Williams. She wanted to return some of the furniture, for it showed little wear, but Mr. Taylor explained that this was no solution.

David often feared that Andy Crutchfield had been right about his having to become the man of the house. He thought he might have to find a second job instead of going back to school in September. A promotion at the plant would increase his pay but he had no chance of getting one.

Mike O'Connor had landed a job in the apprentice program, after David told him about it. In his interview and on his application, he had given David's name as reference. He refused to believe that David had not opened the way for him and used his influence in the personnel office. His expressions of thanks were effusive.

Now that school was out, Andy Crutchfield took steps to bring the son of his friend under his own supervision. David was transferred to the day-shift housekeeping crew.

"I want to help you really learn how to work," Andy Crutchfield told him. "That night-shift crowd is mostly no good—they don't even halfway do what little they supposed to do. I don't blame the lead man 'cause he got nothing to work with. We got good men on my staff, and you can learn. By 'n' by, you develop, learn how to handle yourself on the job, we look for a chance to slip you in on a shop job. You be a helper and learning your skills. You might make a first-rate machinist, same as your daddy was. He'll be proud of you."

There was no point in David's trying to explain what his father had wanted for him. He settled for the time being on making good on the day shift. His own hopes for the future were set aside for the hope of a miracle that would restore his father to full health. Nothing else was as important.

He saw Mike often. They ate together at noon and talked about school, about big league baseball, and about high school football. As Mike talked about football, the plays he had made, the coaching and the team organization at Central, David asked questions. He had not dreamed there were so many things about which he knew so little.

In South Town he and his friends had played football without any professional coaching. His school had not sponsored the team. The principal always said the game was too dangerous. The boys had played hard with substandard equipment and inadequate uniforms. Local merchants were solicited for help, and hats were passed at the games for contributions from the spectators. Broken bones were not infrequent, and though no one David knew had been fatally injured in a game, the threat had always been present

Mike spoke of the strict rules enforced at Central. No player was allowed on the field, even for practice, without full equipment. That was for safety.

He showed with penciled diagrams how complicated patterns of strategy were established. Scrimmage, David learned, was not a hit-and-miss scramble but rather carefully planned drills when each player tried over and over again to perform his own special tasks in order that the team might function properly.

Mike proved to be a good instructor, and David was an eager and willing pupil. Mike brought him books and a football from home. David was fascinated to find that so much information about the game had been reduced to writing. Mike showed him things about handling a ball that he had never heard of. He had never even learned to kick a ball as Mike showed him it should be kicked.

Maybe it was all to the good, he decided, that he had been put off the field before he had had a chance to play that first day at Central. They would have only laughed him off later with his awkward movements and his ignorance of the standard rules. He thought of how ridiculous he must have looked without shoulder guards or a proper-fitting helmet. If the chance should come again—Well, at least he would know more than he had known before.

The hours were long at the plant and the weather was hot, but Mike and David were seldom too tired after work to meet at a playground near the plant for practice.

Some of the men at the plant, Andy Crutchfield among them, thought they were crazy. At the playground the baseball and tennis players stopped to watch the white boy and the colored boy working so earnestly at football. Often they were on the field until dark.

At home David's family settled into an uneasy routine. Mr. Williams seemed to have accepted his role of a sick person. He was passive, rather than cooperative. He spoke slowly; the pitch of his voice was high. There was in everything he said the plaint of a lonesome child. He did what he was told and ate what was put before him. When his sister Mattie returned reluctantly to her home in Richmond, Mr. Williams turned to Betty Jane to fill the place of her aunt. She had always loved her father and admired his strength. She loved him no less in his weakness.

"Pa's kind of asleep," she told her mother, "but I can see he's getting better."

He never seemed to understand about David, and often looked with wonder at this tall young man who called him Pa. He addressed him as David, never calling him son or boy as he had before, and although he watched him, going to work, driving the car, assuming the family responsibilities, he never questioned David. He showed little interest in anything outside his home.

Mrs. Williams was never to forget the way the change came.

One Saturday night when David was out on a date with Jeanette, and Betty Jane was upstairs getting ready for bed, Mrs. Williams left her husband looking at television in the living room. Earlier in the evening she had baked a cake, and now she was ready to start icing it.

"Dear!" She heard him suddenly call in his natural voice.

It frightened her. She started toward the door and saw him coming toward her. His face wore a puzzled frown.

"Dear!" he said again, speaking as he had not for months. "Have I been asleep?"

She went to him. She must not be excited, she told herself, but something inside of her said, "This is your husband."

"Darling!" The word burst from her lips, and then she cried "Oh, thank God!"

He put out his hand, and she took it, lifting it to her face, hardly daring to take him in her arms, fearful that something might happen, that she might be dreaming.

"What is it?" he asked. "What time is it?" He looked around the kitchen as she led him to a chair at the table.

"It's all right, dear. It's all right!" she said.

"But I feel funny. I must have been asleep. I don't remember going to sleep."

Mrs. Williams slipped to her knees beside her husband. "Darling! Ed dear! You've been sick. You've been away. Now you're back—I'm so glad! I'm so thankful!"

He started asking questions, a flood of questions about what had happened.

She was kneeling, trying to answer him and at the same time gasping her thanks. He stood suddenly and spoke. "Hi there, Betty Jane!"

His daughter in her nightgown came running toward him from the hall. She screamed her delight and jumped into his embrace. Mrs. Williams got to her feet. This was the miracle for which they had prayed. This was, at last, the time for which they had waited.

After the first realization of what had happened, Mr. Williams sat as if stunned. His wife was eager to telephone her friends. She knew she should try to locate David, but for a while she could not turn away. There was so much to say, so many things to explain. She told him how long he'd been sick, about the kind doctor, Mattie's visit, David's job, the medical expenses. She soon saw that of his recent experience he could only speak as though he had been dreaming.

Finally she went to the telephone. She did not reach David at the Lenoirs', but she excitedly told Mrs. Lenoir the news; then she called others. They came quickly—the Lenoirs, the Crutchfields, the Taylors, the Reverend Mr. Hayes with his wife, and other friends from the church. When at last David arrived with Jeanette, the house was full.

SIXTEEN

Mr. Williams had been home three and a half weeks when the fog lifted. He was told all that had happened since his collapse two months earlier. With his wife, he went back to the hospital and thanked the doctors and the nurses who had attended him, begging them to forgive him for having been so much trouble. Dr. Meyer was especially delighted and told Mrs. Williams that this case once again supported his theory about the power of certain people to survive.

The doctors examined Mr. Williams at the hospital and found no reason for him to be especially careful. They said he could go back to work and sent a full report to his employers. At the plant, however, it was not easy to convince the medical staff that his recovery was complete. Mr. Williams had to take intelligence tests, psychological tests, and manual dexterity tests. The process took days, but in the end he was allowed to return to his old job, handling the machines he understood so well.

He was very proud of David.

He showed his pride by the way he spoke of his son and by the way he looked at him. He showed it by the way he talked to him, man to man, recognizing that in the family's emergency David had not shirked.

They rode to and from the plant together, with David driving. Some afternoons Mr. Williams came over to the playground and watched Mike put David through his workouts. Other boys had joined them, and a squad was shaping up with Mike as its coach. They did not tackle or block, but they did run signals and practice passing. Mike, who had played at quarterback, was considered especially good at passing. He and David worked hard on pass plays.

"You've got the speed and the ranginess of a good end," he told David. "I never saw anybody at Central who had better hands for receiving. You've really got it, old man."

Although Ed Williams knew very little about football, he felt it would be exciting to see his son play for Central. He did not even consider the thought of David's not going back to school. In fact, he wanted David to leave his job early enough to have a few weeks of vacation before school opened. David thought it might be better for him to stay on as long as possible, for his weekly paychecks were helping to reduce the pile of bills. He was glad, however, when his father insisted that he stop work.

"You know, it's not that I want a vacation," he said, "but football practice starts the twentieth of August. I want to go out for the team. Mike sure has helped me and besides—I see a lot of things different now."

When it was known that David was leaving the plant to go back to school, most of his friends were pleased. The one person who was not was Andy Crutchfield. He thought that David should be grateful for the help his father had given him and that now, with plenty of book-learning in his head, he should turn about and help his father. He had already mentioned David to some of the shop bosses as a good prospect for special training. He told David he was foolish to give up a good job, and he blamed the white boy who was David's friend.

No one was happier than Jeanette. During the summer she and David had not seen much of each other. His football practice had taken up most of his free time, and during the month of August, Jeanette and her sister had gone to visit relatives in New York. David had written to her, and she had responded that despite all the excitement of New York she was anxious to get back to North Town.

The first day of football practice, David sat with the crowd of prospective players that filled the first three or four rows of the stands. The coach told them what he expected of them.

"Some of you men played varsity last year," he said, "and some of you freshmen maybe never had on a football suit before. This you've got to understand. Nobody's got his job with the team sewed up. The men who play will be the ones we—the coaching staff, that is—think are the best, the best players and the best combinations for the time. This means—get it, now—this means if there's a fifteen-year-old freshie who can give more than a letter man in the position, the freshie will play it."

David liked that. He was not sure that he would be as good as Mike said he would, but he was determined to do his best. Now he could believe what the coach was saying. As he looked about him, he did not have his old, uneasy feeling. He no longer felt that the white boys were threatening him.

The coach complained that the turnout was small, though David estimated about a hundred were present. Some of last year's players, like Mike and Buck Taylor, had graduated. Others were still away on their vacations. Alonzo Wells was there, and when they left the stands, David hailed him, and they ran together to the gym.

"I hope some guy doesn't try to play me dirty," Alonzo said in the dressing room.

The remark dampened David's spirits. "This time I think I'll play it different," he told Alonzo. "I've been getting some coaching on the side. I've learned that whatever happens you don't just quit. You keep going forward, pushing, driving."

Alonzo nodded. "That's right," he said. "And you don't lose your head. That's something I ought to remember. Only I just can't stand nobody handing me no stuff. Looks like I always want to get even."

This time David got the correct equipment. The shoes they gave him were too small, but he exchanged them for another player's. He completed his laps easily, and as he circled the field, he thought about the things he had learned that might be helpful the first day.

That evening when Mike phoned him, David could report that the summer coaching had been a big help. The first workout had gone well.

Practice became more strenuous in the days that followed. The coach balanced verbal instruction with demonstration and drill. David was carefully watched. His mistakes were corrected, and occasionally he was complimented.

"Good! Good!" the coach would say. "Only you don't have to drive your man down so hard. This is just for practice."

The coaching staff recognized David's possibilities as an end, and put him with others who were being drilled in broken-field running, pass-receiving, and the running of patterns. He had worked on patterns with Mike, learning to run a planned course, counting the steps, changing directions, holding back until the right instant, and then putting on a burst of speed.

Just beore school started, the squads were organized. The "first thirty-three" was the squad of experienced players. David was on the "second thirty-three," with Alonzo who played halfback. He called David's attention to the fact that Kirinski was a quarterback on the first squad.

"You remember Kirinski," Alonzo said. "That guy we had trouble with last year. Wouldn't pass the ball."

David had almost forgotten Kirinski's name and he was sorry that Alonzo had mentioned it. Here on the field in body-shocking contact he was finding himself thinking less and less about the color and race of those he played with. Alonzo insisted once again that the white boys played dirty against the colored.

"Maybe it just looks that way to you, Al," David said impatiently. "It's a rough game. I guess sometimes they think I'm trying to hurt them. You can't help being hurt sometimes, or hurting the other guy."

"Just watch it," Alonzo warned. "That's all I say. Just watch it!"

David was not looking for trouble. There were times when he recognized unnecessary roughness in a player, but he could not blame the roughness on race prejudice. He himself played a hard game of football.

With the opening of school David was even busier than he had been at the end of the previous semester. Classes and football practice and homework left little time for anything else. He had still not been reclassified as college preparatory, but he had a good selection of classes. Occasionally he went to Jeanette's house to get help with his French, although they found many other things to talk about, too. At home his mother was anxious about his getting hurt in football, but his father was eager for David to make the team, and he promised to come to a game.

By the end of October, Central had played four games and won the first three. The fourth, against a high school in the state capital, they lost by a wide margin.

The next was to be Central's homecoming game against Eastlake, the conference champions of the year before. Eastlake always had heavy teams, and its players were known to be rough.

That week the coach talked to the first and second squads.

"We are not crying over spilt milk," he said, referring to the lost game. "And we're not making excuses. I don't blame anybody more than I do myself, but by the same measure I don't want it to happen again any more than anybody else does.

"Now we're going into high gear to get ready for Eastlake. Nobody's going to be spared. We're going to make changes and use some new plays to meet power with power and make up in skill whatever we may lack in weight."

It was the hardest-driving week of work David had ever known. Taken from the second squad and put with the first, he lined up at left end, ran plays, worked in scrimmage, and sat through hours after dark in skull practice sessions.

The team already had two good ends—the right end better than the left. At right was Fleming, a junior, six feet two and a hundred eighty pounds, fast and good at defense as well as offense. The left end was Anderson, a two hundred pounder, reliable and experienced but without the ability to shift quickly and change course to get out of trouble. The two made a good combination as alternate receivers.

As the coach had them practice, David would not be used for defense. On offense he would be a decoy, a lively threat as alternate pass receiver.

The first day that David worked with the first team Anderson called him aside to show him how to execute a cut. Mike had taught David during the summer, and he knew that the coach liked the way he did it. He watched as Anderson ran through it in a sort of slow motion.

"Try it now," Anderson said. "Just run through it beside me. You'll get it."

"But you're starting your pattern on the wrong foot," David tried to explain. "Look, if I go down here—"

Anderson drew back, his face twisted with scorn. "Wise guy, huh! Now you're showing me! Look, boy! I was playing football when you were down on the plantation picking cotton. You can't tell me how to do anything."

He had not spoken loud, but Fleming and one or two others heard him and frowned. "Take it easy, Anderson," one said.

David tried to put the incident out of his mind. After a while, he decided that Anderson was trying to help. The crack about the cotton fields was ugly, but, after all, it was not far from the truth.

On Friday they ran through their plays in signals without scrimmage and listened to a rundown on Eastlake's formations. An assistant coach read the names of the squad, and David was told to be ready to play. He drew a clean uniform, number 86, reminding himself that it still did not mean he would get in the game.

It was dark when he left the gym. Alonzo was leaving at the same time, and he walked with David to the bus stop.

"It's swell you're with the first string tomorrow," he said.

"Wish me luck," David replied. "I'll probably need it!"

The bus was crowded, and they stood close together

as they rode. David was describing a play he had made during scrimmage when he had tackled and actually brought his man down, when he realized Alonzo was hardly listening.

"I guess you know," Alonzo said, "the quarterback won't be throwing anything good to you."

"Yeah, I guess you're right," David said. "I'll only be in there as a decoy drawing off the Eastlake defense. Maybe they won't throw to me at all."

Alonzo shook his head. "I didn't think you were that dumb," he said. "You know it's that Polack, Kirinski, playing quarter. Man, he'll be throwing the passes and he won't be about to let you get your hands on the ball."

David was annoyed. "Oh, Wells," he said. "You always hang on to that old feeling that Kirinski has something against you. Maybe he did do you dirty one time but you sure squared that with him personally. Besides that was a year ago," he added.

The bus stopped to let off and take on passengers. Alonzo waited until it started again and the sound of the roaring motor muffled his words.

"It's not only Kirinski," he persisted. "It's just about all of them. What about Anderson? Didn't you have trouble with him?"

"That wasn't trouble," David said. "He was trying to show me how to execute. I guess he got hot because I wouldn't listen to him."

"Yeah," Alonzo muttered, "that's about the way I heard it. So you got the regular first-string men down on you, and you think you're going to get a chance? Look man, let's face it. Maybe the coach gives out with all that color-don't-make-no difference business. Maybe he wants to bring you along, but the regulars don't feel the same way. You're new on the team, the quarterback don't like you, and you're black. That's three strikes, anyway you count it. You'll see."

Once home, David was feeling so depressed after his talk with Lonzo that he wanted to call Jeanette. But instead, he called Mike who assured him that he'd get a chance to play and wished him good luck. He said he'd be on the bench, watching.

David did not call Jeanette, for she called him. Happy to know that he would be in uniform, she asked his number. She recognized the concern in his voice and advised him to relax, saying that if he got into the game he would know what to do and if they did not play him this time there would be other chances.

"It's not that exactly," he said. Then he told her about the conversation with Alonzo.

For a while she scolded him. Alonzo, she said, carried a chip on his shoulder. He was suspicious and mean. It was really Alonzo who was prejudiced; with his twisted thinking, he looked for evil.

"Why, I know some of the boys on the team," she said, "and I know they wouldn't be so stupid and vicious as to fail to use a good player simply because of color prejudice. David, you just forget what Alonzo Wells says. Nobody's working against you or Alonzo."

After he left the phone, David told his mother that Jeanette really had a lot of sense.

The game between Central and Eastlake was described in the local newspaper as the classic contest between a good heavy team with power and a good light team with speed.

Saturday the weather was perfect for football, cold with a promise of snow in the air. It was bright and clear in the morning, but shortly after midday, clouds shut out the sun. The game was to be played in the city's Memorial Park, and at the kickoff, all twelve thousand seats were filled. Station WNOR carried the broadcast.

Choosing to receive, Eastlake made four first downs without losing the ball. Shifting the line first to right and then to left and keeping Central off balance, they went over the goal line after four minutes of play. They missed the place kick, and the score held at 6–0 at the end of the quarter, with Eastlake on Central's eight-yard line. At the beginning of the second quarter, Eastlake threw a pass into the end zone, scoring their second touchdown of the game. This time they made their conversion with a place kick, and the score stood 13–0 for the rest of the half. Eastlake tried passing again, but Central was ready for them.

In the locker room between halves, the coach made the men know that the game was by no means lost. Central had plenty of stuff left, he insisted, and when the team ran out on the field at the sound of the horn for the second half, David had no doubt that his big chance would be coming up soon. He was in perfect physical condition, but he was tense. In the pit of his stomach, he felt empty. The coach motioned him to take a place near him on the bench. He moved over and waited. Watching with the others, his own body moving with the plays, he forgot his tenseness and his emptiness. He felt as if he were already in the game.

Five minutes of the third quarter had gone by when Central recovered the ball, following a fumble by Eastlake on its own forty-yard line. It was then that Coach Henderson pulled six men off the field, and David was sent in to replace Anderson at left end. Fleming was at right end; Kirinski was at quarterback. In the huddle, Kirinski called the play. David was to run his pattern, Kirinski to pass, Fleming to receive. The signals were called; the ball was snapped. David ran straight ahead, then left three steps and right three steps, and then down the field with only a glance back to see the ball sailing toward Fleming. Another glance, and he saw the safety man on top of Fleming bat the ball from his outstretched hands. David had done his part as a decoy. Two of Eastlake's men had gone for him.

"This we got to make good," Kirinski said in the huddle. He called for a short pass, and David knew he was to run a side-line post. At the signal, he ran his pattern and Fleming ran his. The ball never came. Kirinski fumbled, and the ball got away from him. There was a pile up, but when it was cleared, a Central halfback had possession. For the third down, Kirinski called for repetition of the long pass play, the ball to go to Fleming, with David running as decoy and alternate pass receiver.

Again David took his place. Signals were called, and at the snap of the ball he started down the field, running his diagonals at three-quarter speed. He saw Eastlake's safety man close on Fleming's heels. Then he saw the ball arch high in the air and come over his own path, but so far ahead! His eyes fixed on the ball, he increased his speed. He had to be there before it came down. He was gaining, and then his hands went up together, and at last his fingers touched the ball, and he was pulling it in and tucking it into the tight crevice between his arm and his ribs. His speed did not slacken. He had the happy sensation of flying, not knowing that his feet touched ground. He saw the goal posts ahead, and the bar above as though they were moving toward him, and then he was running across diagonal lines and knew he was in the end zone.

When Kirinski reached him, he slapped David enthusiastically on the back. "Good going, Williams!" He grinned. "I knew you could make it!"

Central converted with a neat place kick, making the score 13 to 7 as the timekeeper's gun fired to signal the end of the quarter.

In the fourth quarter when Central got the ball, David was again sent in on offensive. Kirinski kept the game open with passing, double reverses, and all the fancy plays Central had developed to use against the heavier team. They went on to another touchdown, this time with Fleming carrying. They made the conversion, running the score to 14–13, and the stands went wild.

As David ran off the field, after the second touchdown, he saw Mike jumping up and down on the coach's bench with excitement. He grabbed David, hugged him, and pounded his back.

"Baby," he shouted, "you did it! You did it! I saw you

making those patterns. It was beautiful. I told you all the time. I told you!"

Buck Taylor was there, too; less noisy, he shook David's hand. "You're all right, Williams," he said heartily. "They've been telling me about you. You're all right."

Alonzo Wells was waiting with a blanket for David. As he wrapped it around him and led him to a seat on the bench, he said softly, "You know Kirinski never meant you to get that pass. He thought he was throwing the ball away. You fooled him, but good!"

Sitting shapeless in his blanket on the side lines, in the final minutes of the game, David for the first time thought about the people in the stands. Now he heard their cheers. He turned and looked up at the crowd. The playing field was in shadow but the late afternoon sun had broken through the clouds, lighting a row of American flags silhouetted against the sky. David knew that his father was there, and Jeanette. Principal Hart would be in the crowd, and his teachers. Yes, and Jimmy Hines and his unhappy friends. He could not pick out the faces, white or black or brown, but he knew they were all there. This, he thought, was like America.

As he turned back toward the playing field, a great joy came over him. He knew he was part of Central's team. He did not think of himself as a Negro but as a student of North Central High School who had shared with others in gaining a hard-fought victory.

He was never to forget that scene.

SEVENTEEN

AFTER THE EXCITEMENT OF THE GAME, the wild cheering of the spectators, the victorious rush of the team, and the noisy confusion of the showers and the locker room, David's ride homeward with his father was very quiet.

Mr. Williams had brought the car from the parking lot to the exit nearest the team's quarters under the stands. He watched as the players came out in bursts of twos and threes, calling final farewells before going their several ways.

David came out with such a group. He opened the car door and called back, "See you Monday, Kirinski!" But Mr. Williams was already in the passenger's seat, so David went around to the other side.

"Hi, Dad!" he said. "So you saw a real football game!"

"I sure did," his father said, reaching over to slap

David on the knee. "Boy, your ma should've been here. Or maybe it was better she wasn't here. I guess she would have busted wide open with her pride. I 'most did myself."

David maneuvered the car through the heavy traffic, content to let his father talk.

"I knew when you first ran out there something was going to happen."

"But, Pa," David objected, "you got to remember it was all the team, not just me."

"Yeah, I know that," Mr. Williams agreed. "But man alive! Look like I knew you'd make good—and when you was splitting down there and the ball was going over your head—I knew you'd make it, but I prayed anyway. Yes, sir! I jumped up and hollered, 'God help him!' I said it right out loud—'God help him!' "

David laughed. "Well, I guess that was what gave me that extra boost—'cause I mighty near didn't get there."

"But you know when I was praying I wasn't worried," his father insisted. "I just knew you'd make it!"

"You can't always be sure, Pa," David replied. "There's so much more goes into it—all the other players and then you have the other team, too."

"But irregardless to all that, some things you know—" Pa stopped for a minute. "It's like seeing you grow up and taking your place on your school team—and like even taking over the driving while your pa just sits up and rides."

"I like to drive, Pa. Hope I don't scare you too much."

"You don't," Mr. Williams said emphatically. "You're a

good driver, but just the same I feel like I got to help you. Sometimes I most shove my foot through the floor helping you put on brakes. When you get your own home and you have a son nearly grown and driving for you, you'll see what I mean." Then he added, "Or maybe it will be your private plane, and your boy will be piloting you to visit the old folks at home."

"Wait, Pa! Me with a plane of my own?"

"Why not? When I was your age I guess my pa didn't imagine me having my own car, and I guess there are as many planes now as there were cars in those days. Down around our section, folks were still using wagons and plowing with mules almost altogether. Why, I can remember the first car I ever rode in.

"First time I ever rode in one I was going to the old Boydton Institute. It was a church school where they used to have nothing but missionary teachers. It was while I was going there they had the first colored principal, man named Dr. Morris. I was on my way to school one morning when his son came along, driving the principal's car. His name was Satchel. He already had a load of boys on board, but he stopped and I got on, too. I remember Andy Crutchfield's brother was one of them."

David tried to imagine the thrill for a country boy of riding in a car for the first time.

"That day in chapel," Mr. Williams went on, "the principal, this Dr. Morris, talked about what we could do when we grew up. He was a good man, and all the people thought a lot of him. He said that we could do anything we wanted to, with God's help. He said we could be anything we wanted to be. I'll never forget how I felt. He asked us to decide what we wanted to do with ourselves, and then he called on us to stand up when we'd made up our minds.

"I decided I would be a mechanic, and that I would have my own automobile, and I stood right up and looked at him. I think I was in third grade, though I was about twelve years old. I was way down front when I stood up, and somebody laughed, but I didn't turn around.

"Then Dr. Morris prayed that God would bless our lives, and, say, if ever I felt like a prayer went home, that one did. When it was over, I looked around and I was the only one standing, but I knew from then on, I was going to be a mechanic, and a good one. That Dr. Morris was a fine man."

David slowed down the car for the left turn into Twenty-fourth Street. He waited for the traffic to pass. He knew that his father had achieved his boyhood ambition. Maybe the praying of the principal had helped. He saw a break in the line of cars, and he swiftly crossed the street.

"That's the way I used to feel about being a doctor, Pa," he said.

"What do you mean 'used to'?" Mr. Williams asked.

"Well, I know now that it's terribly expensive, and it's a lot harder and takes a lot more time than I used to figure."

"O.K., so it won't be easy. It wasn't easy for us to leave down South and get started here—and it wasn't easy for you to get on the team and make that touchdown today. It costs more, and it's harder to get, but if God spares you and gives you health, I don't see any reason why you can't make it. I promise you, I'll do my part."

David swung the car in from the street and stopped in the driveway. For a minute Mr. Williams did not move. David cut the motor and waited.

His father spoke again. "Dr. Williams." He was looking at David, not speaking to him really, just thinking out loud. "David Andrew Williams, M.D."

Afterword

When I was young, I didn't know my father was a great writer. During my early years, he worked as a teacher and a social worker; and I recall how he would often come home after a long day's work and sit at his desk far into the night, working on his books and stories. It was not until years later that I began to realize the magic he created on his typewriter.

Lorenz Graham was a pioneer in children's literature. He was the first African American writer to portray African Americans realistically in his books. Books had been written about well-known African American heroes and heroines, and other books had been written portraying blacks as deprived and hopeless. But my father took a completely different approach in his books.

He felt America should know about the lives and experiences of ordinary African Americans. So he wrote about a young man and his family—a family who struggled hard to overcome the injustices and hardships of the troubled times in which they lived. The Williams family was courageous and strong. In spite of all the problems they encountered, they never lost hope that the future would be better.

My father's readers enjoyed these novels about David Williams and his family. After each of the books reached the public, he received letters from people asking him to write another book because they wanted to know what happened to David next. Thus, the "Town" novels developed, spanning several decades in the life and experiences of David Williams.

The books in this series brought numerous honors and awards to my father. His greatest satisfaction, however, came from spreading his message that when people of different backgrounds understand one another, there is greater opportunity to achieve peace and harmony in the world.

Ruth Graham Siegrist, Ph.D.